*Aaron "Silky" Allen*

*Presents*

# CONFESSIONS OF A JACKBOY

By

*Aaron "Silky" Allen*

This book is dedicated to:

To all the real ones incarcerated across the U.S. --- keep your head up and your eyes open. To Laton Cunningham…RIP--- to Mark (Mo) Brock, and the other Mark, WB (James Harrell), Face (Cedric Muldrow), Silk (Anthony R.), SP (Sherrone Greene), Big O (Orlando C.), Kerry Dale (Young World), Mosheh(Mo), Jessie Bracey, Mac10 (Jesse M.), Church Boy (Brandon C.), Penny (Ivan M.), Waldo (Valdo), Bushaun (Rodney Jones), Daniel Stancil (Charlie/LA), Orlando O. (Double-O from Shelby), Larry Leggett (L), James Anderson (Bert), Raleigh Red, ScootieMac, Willie Jackson and any of the Real Ones I may have forgotten. I also say keep your head up and your eyes open.

This book is also dedicated to Me. I worked damn hard---really. Pat on the back to me, Struggle Street Publishing and BMDS Barbering/ VIP Mobile Spa Service and to all those that have loyally supported me and my aspirations. AARON ALLEN FILMS next level---about to bring my words to life.

To my son, Dareon--- I am trying to create and leave you a legacy as great as Chester Himes or Sir Donald Goines. Do not be discouraged. Continue to be the brilliant and beautiful you.

To Nutcha, Squeak, Joe Rockhead and Aquaman--- be great, every day.

To Taurus "Ty" Watkins, Clary D., Corey Collins, Gator (Donald) Brown, Leon Allen, Sam Allen, Haul Allen, Fox Allen, Charles Lee Allen (RIP), Rasheen "Shiesty" Massey, Dominique McDonald, D. Hailey, Jermaine Hailey, Curt R., Chancy (Cuda Face), Todd & Linda, Jamie B., L. Carelock (RIP), L. Byrd (RIP), Lee Blount, L. Hamilton, Preston P. Johnson, R. Barrino, Clipper Game (Rome), Damon (Big D) Thomas, HTG, Walt B., Allan Carson, Jimmy from the Struggle (RIP)…the stories of you are legendary. To the South Side of Monroe

(NC)---we can do better, respectfully. Free all political prisoners---it's all politics(politricks).

To the ghost skins and concealers-of-racism, your hate can not extinguish my black brilliance. To the crooked judicial officials, malfeasant prosecutors and undertrained, overzealous police that strive daily to dismantle black excellence and destroy black and brown lives, may God smite you. Stop playing on our intelligence, either we all do right, or we all do wrong---it can't continuously be bias. Enough plutocracy and white privilege. Our Blackness is not criminal---yet you persecute us like the living Gods that we are. I stay aware of your misdeed and malfeasance---my grandmother Ruby put me up on game a long time ago and my Pops (Karo) told me ***never take any wooden nickels.***

In memory of Eddie Gingham, whom I affectionately called, "Cornbread Son" ---he hated and loved it simultaneously. I hope you found solace and bliss. Just wish you would have chosen another alternative.

In memory of Jessica Mitchell.

Long Live Julius "Juice" Sampson, Jr.

Free Rob C.     Free Gotti   Free Mark Brock   Free WB   Free the Guys

# Table of Contents

## Introduction

I appreciate each one of you taking the time and opportunity to purchase and read my literary work. Thank you.

This work will grab you---shake you with harsh and violent realities' that make up every epic tale. Horrific, real, and racy. Not every horror story consists of ghost or zombies---at least not these.

*Jackboy-* (noun) a person or thief who commits robberies, usually violent in nature. A **jackboy**, although having a predatory nature is a victim of poverty and systematic social ills---normally the underlined reasons for said robberies and acts of violence. If you know nothing about street life prepare to be frightened. Enjoy.

# Chapter One: In Real Life

"Hurry up *an'* close the door! It's *col'* as hell out *dhere!*" Tasia exclaimed, sitting on the loveseat in a grey Victoria's Secret boy-beater and pink terry cloth short-shorts. Her lithe, caramel legs tucked beneath her derriere as she fidgeted with the white trim on her shorts. Her orders had been directed at her best friend---Erica.

Erica Claiborne was growing sick of Tasia's *shit*. The twenty-year-old, single mother of two had felt like a mother of four ever since she had invited Tasia Gaskin and her fourteen-month-old son, Omarion to stay with her three weeks ago. The reason being--- Tasia, who had been two months behind in her rent and on the verge of eviction had set her apartment on fire and made it look like an accident, so that she could receive assistance from Red Cross. The organization had put her and her and her infant son up in the Motel 6 for three days, given her an emergency EBT card, vouchers for clothing and hygiene products.

Tasia, affectionately known as "Tay", the conniving, project-raised, nineteen-year-old, sponsor-seeker that she was had introduced the items to the *Street Exchange* --- she had made grocery purchases with her EBT card for low-level dope boys in exchange for cash. With the Wal-Mart vouchers she had purchased bras, panties, sexy lingerie, and a few articles of sleep wear for her son--- she had utilized the hotel stay but had convinced her youthful-looking mother to keep her son while she sucked and fucked for three days. Along with the possession she had removed from the apartment the night before the fire.

Erica slammed the door of her Section 8 sponsored apartment and placed her hands on her wide, designer denim-covered hips. Shopping bags dangling from her fingers. Even angry she was adorable--- a modish, raspberry-highlighted mohawk, shimmery lip gloss and beautiful, flawless dark chocolate skin. Despite having pushed two children from her womb. Erica's five-three, one hundred- and seventy-one-pound frame was curvaceous and very desirable.

"*Ooooh!* I knew it! I knew it---talked all that shit! You are the father!" Tasia screamed at the T.V. screen as the skinny figure on the stage dressed in oversized clothing dropped his head into his lap.

Erica looked around the living room, not able to comprehend why her living room was a mess--- toddler toys, large crayons, coloring books and children clothing cluttered the floor, chair and couch.

"Tay---what the hell you been *doin'* all day?" Erica's tone was vexed.

Tasia rolled her eyes, smacked her readily moist lips and folded her arms across her petite frame. "I fed the kids," she answered dryly.

"It's damn near two-thirty! You ain't been feeding them for four hours!"

"Okay! Damn, Erica!" Tasia blurted as she leapt from the loveseat and began picking up items. "You act like you somebody momma---always *fussin'* about nothing."

"Where my babies?" Erica asked, ignoring her friend's griping.

"*Sleepin'.*"

"Sleeping? They were just waking up when I was leaving."

"Yeah, now they on nap time. I'm running this shit like a real daycare center," Tasia explained.

"Well, they clean up at a real daycare," Erica retorted as she proceeded down the hall towards the bedroom.

"Damn! *I'mma* clean up, Erica. You act like I'm *yo' fuckin'* maid!"

Erica stopped in midstride. "No! I'm actin' like you don't pay no damn bills around here," she said matter-of-factly before continuing towards the children's room.

"Bitch, I know you *ain't trippin' 'bout* no money--- I get my check today. I'm just waiting on my momma to call an' let me know when it gets there. I'll give you some *fuckin'* money!"

Erica hated when Tasia's voice became irritably whiney. She really hated her personality in general---she was manipulative, talkative, two-faced and trifling. And she was way too promiscuous.

"I ain't ask you for no money! I asked you to keep the place clean, you know Taco coming by---nasty bitch," Erica muttered.

"I heard you!" Tasia yelled down the hallway in laughter in laughter. Erica herself broke into laughter. She investigated the bedroom on the left and found all three kids on the bed in a heap of arms and feet sleeping soundly. She then thought about the fathers of her two children---her two-year-old child, D'Eric was Dewayne's son. Dewayne was a deadbeat, nothing more than a sperm donor---he had only seen his son twice. One of those visits had been nothing more than a poor attempted to get into Erica's panties.

Nerica. Her fourteen-month-old daughter was Nathan's child. Nathan had been a father to his daughter and Erica's son for the moment he was there. Despite their relationship he had even been somewhat of a father to Erica, but now the thirty-two-year-old hustler was twelve months into his two-hundred-and-thirty-month prison sentence. Out of adoration for the man he had been before his incarceration Erica wrote him from time to time, sent an occasional money order through JPay and accepted his collect calls.

Poor, little, Omarion---she looked at the sleeping bastard sadly. Tasia, her promiscuity her curse, was unaware of who her child's father was, she had slept with so many men around the time of conception that Maury could have run a weeklong paternity special on her alone.

always arrived with bass-driven music blaring from his lowrider truck---he never blew the horn, never got out and knocked on the door.

"Invite him in! And I told you 'bout that burrito shit!" She responded curtly as she closed the door to the children's bedroom which was also where Tasia slept. She hurried to her own bedroom to put away the shopping bags from Belk's and Lady Foot Locker.

"Get out and bring yo' ass in!" Tasia yelled, standing on her tiptoes with the front door wide open. The cold air pulling her nipples away from her aureoles beneath the cotton boy-beater.

Tasia barely made room for the cherubic Mexican to amble past as he entered the apartment, a small backpack on his shoulder. Their eyes met, Taco, just a few inches taller than her, smiled as his hand grazed her thigh.

Erica and Taco's relationship was not as serious as Taco would have liked, but even if it was Tasia was not going to a *d-boy* and that's all she cared about.

"Have a seat---she'll be out in a minute," she said pleasantly as she went back to straightening up the living room. The chubby drug dealer sat and watched intently as Tasia seduced him, bending over to pick up toys while turning her ass in his direction.

"You need some help?" Taco asked, his throaty accent strangling his English.

"I can handle it," she replied. Looking back over her shoulder. It was evident from the pubic hair peeking out of her shorts that she was not wearing any panties. Taco shifted uncomfortably in his seat.

"Did you wash your ass?" Erica asked abruptly, startling them both. Their eyes bulging with guilt as they stared at her.

"Yeah, I washed my ass! I wash my ass *er'day*!" Tasia said defensively. She hated how

Erica crept into a room.

"Okay---cool. Then how about *washin'* that ring out my tub." Erica's tone was dry. Tasia's caramel cheeks became flushed with embarrassment---she stormed down the hall towards the children's room with her arms full of toys and clothes. Then a door slammed. "Don't be stupid, Taco."

"What *cho* talking about?" He chuckled.

"You know what the fuck I'm talkin' about. Fuck that bitch you want to."

"*Cho* trippin'."

"Okay--- I'm just *lettin'* you know," she said solemnly.

Taco exhaled loudly, placed the backpack at his feet and fished from it a compressed cellophane-wrapped package containing nine ounces of cocaine---*fishscale.* Then three large Mason jars, each containing a containing a pound of high-grade marijuana. Erica pulled a bankroll from the pocket of her jeans and tossed it into his lap, before placing the product on the coffee table.

"What's *dis*? *Dis* ain't nothin' but five-gees," he answered with frustration, having counted the money twice.

"Yeah, that's for the coke."

"Okay---but what about the weed?"

"I owe you forty-five *hunned.* You been *frontin'* me weed, why you *gonna* stop now," Erica argued.

"Because you been hustling for a minute now---you don't need me to front you nothin'. It's bad enough I'm *lettin' cho* get it for the low---that's Kush, it ain't no homegrown."

"That's how you treat your girl?" Erica asked, pouting her lips as she sat on Taco's lap. He exhaled again.

"Oh, you're my girl when you need *somethin'*---but when I need something you don't know me," he said vehemently.

"What you need?" She said batting her eyelashes enticingly as she wiggled on his lap, arousing him.

"You know what I need," he growled as he caressed her thick thighs with his pudgy fingers.

"We *gonna* get together---but not today." She looked at him with pleading eyes as she eased of his lap.

"You been *runnin'* that same game for the last three weeks. I'll be by here Monday for the rest of my money," Taco stated coldly as he got up and made his way towards the front door.

"You ain't gotta act like that," Erica insisted. Her own agitation building. Taco said nothing, slamming the door as he exited.

"Tay! Tay! I need you in the kitchen---we gotta cook an' bag up this shit!" Erica commanded as she moved the product to the tiny kitchen.

Tasia gaited into the kitchen displaying as much attitude as she could muster---still upset by her friend's comments. She rolled her eyes at Erica before making her way to the cabinet for the needed utensils---a box of sandwich bags, a cigarette lighter and two tiny digital scales. From a small box atop the refrigerator, she retrieved a pack of Game Sliver cigars, sat down at the dining table. Except for the blunt which she skillfully tore open with manicured thumbnail---she unscrewed the top from one of the Mason jars, pinched a plentiful portion of the yellow and purple-haired bud that resembled a Laker, and began crumbling and lining it across the cigar leaf. The smell pungent, yet therapeutic.

Once she had the Game packed and rolled, she deep throated the blunt, sealing it with her sickly-sweet saliva. Then she dried it with the flame from the lighter before placing it to her lips and setting fire to the opposite end---she took a long, hard toke before releasing a cloud of thick smoke.

The expression on Erica's face was sickly. "I don't even know if I wanna hit that now. You did all that *freakin'* shit to it---and why you think you gotta fire up a blunt every time we get ready to bag up or cook something?" She asked as she watched Tasia hit the blunt for a fourth time.

"*Sheeiiit*, this right here---get me focused. I can go in now," Tasia answered with a giggle as she passed the blunt and began weighing and bagging the potent marijuana.

Erica turned on the stove and got out a Pyrex pot before she sat down and took a toke from the blunt---then another, and another, before coughing lightly.

"Give me a shotgun," Tasia blurted. Erica obliged as her friend inhaled the Kush smoke while continuing to weigh and bag the herb. Abruptly the phone rang. "Get that! That's probably my momma---if it is, tell her we'll be there in an hour."

"I'm *goin'* to the hospital," Tashay announced as she entered the room. Interrupting their frivolous debate.

"Damn---bought you a house in Virginia, huh?" Sleepy asked humorously.

"Go to hell," she replied dryly.

Corey looked at them both puzzled. "What---what I miss?"

"House-In-Virginia," Axe stated slowly. His brow raised anticipating Corey's comprehension of the phrase.

"Da clown tryna say I got HIV," Tashay blurted. "Anyway--- I'm goin' to the hospital to see Natasha---she had her baby."

"Tell her I said, good push," Sleepy said. They all burst into laughter, except for Man--- he never laughed, barely talked.

"You stupid!" Tashay cackled. She then kissed Axe on the cheek. The two were the epitome of an odd couple. Axe---Alexander Wilson was twenty-one and was as black as the ace of spades. He had never finished school and was an ex-convict and career criminal who had spent sixty-four months in the Department of Corrections. Tashay Massey was a junior college graduate, a twenty-two-year-old, senior-level manager at a consultant firm and her skin was fair that she was practically an albino.

"Ay---Tashay!" Sleepy yelled as she made her way to the door. "You didn't give me a kiss." Tashay gave him the middle finger instead before exiting the apartment.

"But like I was sayin'--- Solange look better than Beyonce, an' she real. She smokes weed and she got pregnant when she was still a teenager," Axe stated with conviction. "Her last release was way better than that Sasha bullshit, *muthaphukkaz* just slept on it."

"That last release was her last release." Laughter erupted.

"Anyway, her ass ain't fatter than Beyonce!" Corey responded.

"It *ain't* fatter than Kash Doll's, but Rihanna look better than all of 'em!" Sleepy exclaimed.

"Rihanna can't dance!" Corey insisted.

"All you care about is a fat ass, fuck what *dhey* face look like." Axe said before taking a swig of his Hennessy and Coke.

"You the same way." Corey said as he passed the blunt to Man.

"How you figure?"

"*'Cause* Tashay got that fat ass, and she don't look all that in the face," he said before dropping his gaze to the floor.

"*Whoooa!*" Sleepy blurted as he put a fist to his mouth to conceal his laughter. Man shook his head in disbelief.

"I didn't mean it like that, Axe---Tashay cute, but she ain't no Beyonce."

"You need to shut the fuck up, real talk. And yo' fat ass ain't no Jay-Z and Jay a funny *lookin' muthafukka*," Axe said curtly before changing the subject. "Ay! *Dhere* he go!"

All four men watched through the open blinds as the young hustler draped in jewels exited the adjacent apartment complex. Ralph brushed lint from his Amiri jeans, blew a kiss to his mistress and moved swiftly to the classic 1979 Cadillac Deville. The car with its cottonwood green paint job had the appearance that it was wet, its gleaming **elbows**, or rather, wire-rims from a 1984 Cadillac, accentuated the Vogue *tyres* with their mustard and mayonnaise-colored walls. Chrome gleamed from every angle of the vehicle.

"We'll be back---come on Sleepy," Axe commanded.

Ralph pulled out of the driveway and cruised to the stop sign--- Young Dolph and Key Glock's "Rain Rain", blaring from the car's five-thousand-dollar stereo system.

"Ay---Ralphie!" Axe yelled, throwing up both arms. "What it do?"

Ralph contemplated whether he should drive on, but he did not want to seem disrespectful considering Axe was casually approaching the driver's side of his vehicle. He knew he was out of his element---he was from Camp Sutton, but he found the women on the Southside to be more ample in the derriere region and more into pleasing their men.

"Ain't nothin'." He replied nervously, trying to speak over Dolph's inspirational verse. He unconsciously caressed his chains. Ralph was way too familiar with Axe's means of hustle---two members of his clique had previously fell victim to Axe's armed robbery skills. In one heist he had pilfered twelve thousand dollars and three kilos of cocaine with seventy-two percent purity. Which is how Ralph believed Tashay was able to afford her new BMW.

Ralph saw no sign of  Sleepy---Axe's ever present crime partner, so he figured he would be safe.

"Can I be like you when I grow up?" Axe asked, flexing the muscles concealed by his black thermal shirt. He was a master of flattery, able to *rock anyone to sleep.*

"Shoot, man---I'm just *livin'.*" Ralph said exhaustedly. His mannerisms were false, and Axe quickly recognized Ralph's attempt to keep the cheat off himself.

"You livin' major---big boy ride, girl got that big ass! You got it!" Axe teased. The hustler forced a laugh, his face bore a look of pain that was prophetic.

"Where ya boy?" Ralph asked, adjusting the Rolex on his wrist. No doubt a pill-poppers heirloom-stolen-pawn shop pawn-off never picked up.

"Right here, playboy." Sleepy said coolly from the passenger seat of the Cadillac. Ralph turned to the right with a look of fear and disappointment on his face. Sleepy let the Walther .45 semiautomatic rest against the hustler's temple like an exhausted track star.

"Man damn!" Ralph exclaimed with frustration. He despised Sleepy for no other reason than that he was a pretty boy pretending to be a thug. His hands went to his lap. Desperation---which Sleepy quickly recognized. The pistol slammed into Ralph's skull. Blood began to leak from the gash above his right eye.

Sleepy tilted Ralph's head. "Bleed on that Vlone hoodie---don't bleed on the seat, nigga. And that chick you just dropped off better had gave you crabs. What you *diggin'* in *yo'* shit for?!" Sleepy asked as he fondled the young hustler roughly. "Ay, Axe---he gotta gun."

"He had a gun. Let me see."

Sleepy passed the handgun through the driver side window as if Ralph was non-existent. "*Oooh,* it looks new. I *gots* to have this." Axe insisted. Sleepy looked vexed at the statement.

"How much paper you got?" Sleepy snarled, aiming the gun at his nostril. Ralph felt his urethra loosening and his bladder weakening.

Ralph frowned. "*I'on't* know--- *'bout* four bands."

"Four bands?! Damn---shorty got you *tippin'* heavy! Sex like that?"

"*Nah*---I *ain't goin'* for that Sleepy! He *sittin'* on some paper!" Axe growled.

Violently and abruptly, Ralph found the car door open and himself on the asphalt. His left elbow scraped and bleeding. Axe stood over him, pistol in his hand and hate in his eyes.

"Get naked!" Axe yelled.

"What?!" Ralph exclaimed.

Axe fired a round into the black tar pavement next to Ralph's legs. The bullet fracturing the pavement sent hot sand and stone shards into Ralph's forearm. "Get naked, nigga!"

## Chapter Two: Axe a Fool

"It's your boss lady---Angie. She wants to know if you wanna work tomorrow," Erica said as she walked into the kitchen on her iPhone. Angie was the manager at Sonic's, the fast-food eatery where Tasia worked part-time. The job was necessary to her financial situation---as part of former president Clinton's welfare reform. Tasia had to work a job to receive government assistance. Truth is, she barely worked---one of the perks of carrying on a lesbian affair with the manager.

"Tell her I'll call her back an' let her know," Tasia said as she continued bagging up the marijuana.

"She'll call back." And with push and beep of a button she hung up the phone. As she went to place it on the table it rung again. "Hello?"

"It's your momma," Erica announced, handing her the phone as she sat down.

"Uh-huh. Yeah--- we'll be over there in a lil' bit, so have me a plate ready. I know you fixed somethin' good. Okay. Bye." Tasia placed the phone on the table and started laughing.

"What's so funny?"

"I was just *thinkin'* about Taco *tryna* fuck you from the back an' he got dicky-do," Tasia explained with more marijuana induced laughter.

"Dicky-do? What the hell is dicky-do?" Erica had a look of bewilderment on her deep brown face.

"That's when his belly sticks out more than his dicky-do."

Tasia was now laughing hysterically, and it was infectious. "You know you wrong for that," Erica laughed, doubling over in her seat. When she looked up, she was face to face with Nerica---she stood knock-kneed in her yellow pajamas with the attached feet, rubbing her always wandering green eyes. Looking more and more like her father with each passing day---amber skin, thick lashes, and sandy-brown hair.

"*Hey-y-y-y*! Pretty girl! *Whatcha doin'* up?"

"I heard laugh-in'."

"I heard laugh-in'" Erica mimicked jovially. Nerica laughed as she snuggled into her mother's arms.

"You need to hurry *an' cook up* that shit, so you can take me to my momma's," Tasia instructed. Interrupting the mother and daughter moment.

"Mom-my, can I help cook?" Nerica asked with sheer innocence. Erica gave her friend a look of disgust before calming her expression for the sake of her child. "No baby---you *cain't* help mommy right now, but you can later, *okay*?"

"Okay." She smiled, revealing only a few teeth, her eyes sparkling.

"Go wake up D'Eric and Omarion, baby."

The man-made material that made up the soles of Nerica's pajamas slapped the tile-floor as she scurried down the hall to the bedroom.

"Don't be talking 'bout this shit in front of my baby," Erica said dryly. "What the fuck wrong *wit'* you?"

"What's wrong with me? Bitch---you the one got the shit sittin' out for her to see it!"

"Okay, but I ain't talkin' about it, Tay."

"I'm finished," Tasia said rubbing the marijuana residue from her hands as she stood. "I'm goin' to put on some clothes and then I'll be ready."

The iPhone rang as Tasia was sauntering down the hall to the children's room. Erica answered on the second ring. "Ay, Theresa---call me right back on my cell, I'm doin' something so *I'ma* put you on speakerphone. No bitch---you stupid and you nasty. Just call me back, bye."

Memphis rapper, Juicy J's voice proclaimed an attitude as Erica pried the tiny cellphone from her pocket. She tapped the speaker button and placed the phone on the counter as she moved back to the stove where a pot of water continued boiling, a box of baking soda and an empty baby food jar sat to the side---along with a tray of melting ice and a spoon. "What the business is?" She asked.

"The business is Sleepy and Axe at it again. Excuse me---Axe the Great. That's what he callin' *his-self* now. Anyway ---they robbed Ralph, *gurl!*" Theresa informed her friend.

"*Stopppppit!*"

"*Forreal*! Robbed his cute ass in broad daylight! Stripped him naked in the middle of the street---and he *holdin', guuurl.*"

"What was he holding?" Erica was intrigued, patting her head gently as she listened. The hair-gel beginning to irritate her scalp.

"Money and jewelry! But I'm talking about he was holdin'---and you know it's cold as fuck outside! The big dick energy is real!"

"You was out there when it happened?"

"No, but NeNe told me. She was at Mary Anne's getting her hair did," Theresa said matter-of-factly. She had a habit of telling a story as if was there.

"NeNe?" Erica exclaimed. "I thought Mary Anne said she wasn't fuckin' with that bitch no more *'cause* the last time she came and got her hair done---she paid her and then stole the money back."

"Yeah, yeah--- she said all that, but come to find out Turtle, her dope *smokin'*-ass, baby-daddy stole the money!"

"You *lyin'*!" Erica blurted as she measured out four grams of cocaine.

"No, I ain't. Let me finish---while Mary Anne was outside talking to somebody in a burgundy car, NeNe was in the bathroom getting her back blown out by the crackhead!" Theresa burst into laughter. Erica remained silent for a few seconds. Dumbfounded by the chain of events.

"Was you there?"

"No, but Tangela told me," Theresa explained.

"Tangela was there?"

"No, but NeNe told her what happened ---you know NeNe ain't gonna tell me she fucked Mary Anne's man, if that's what you wanna call him. I think they was doin' more than fuckin' in that bathroom. I think that NeNe might be *smokin'*, why else would you fuck a crackhead, unless you a crackhead *yo' self*."

"So, you *sayin'* Mary Anne *smokin'*, too?"

"It is what it is---shit---she pop pills." Theresa said dryly.

"*Woooow*! You wrong for that." Erica said laughing loudly.

"No, I'm real for that."

"Finish telling me 'bout Ralph," Erica commanded, her frustration evident.

"Oh, yeah---they stripped him ass-naked, robbed him right in front of Axe's girlfriend's crib."

"Who?!" Erica blurted with eagerness.

"Tashay---you know them black-ass *niggaz* like 'em light, bright and damn near white." Both women laughed. "They say they got like twelve racks."

"Twelve *baaaaand*! Why the hell was he was he *walkin'* around Hudson Street with twelve bands?" Erica asked excitedly as she dumped two tablespoons of baking soda into the jar with the coke. Not able to understand the mindset of today's hustlers. "Ralph ain't even from the Southside---what the fuck was he doin' on this side anyway?"

Theresa snorted loudly. "He wasn't walking, he was *drivin'* his Cadillac. And Sharon---he was *leavin'* her house," she answered.

"You *talkin'* about big-butt big lip Sharon?!"

"Nasty! Look, Theresa---I'ma have to call you back, okay? I gotta take Tay by her momma's."

"Oh, oh, okay. Call me." Theresa insisted before hanging up. Erica pressed the **END** button on her phone then proceeded to cook up the coke. Two small boulders of congealed cocaine lay drying on wax paper on the kitchen table. Once she was finished, she cleaned up and headed back towards the bedrooms.

Erica was devasted by what she saw---her mouth open as she stood in front of her children's room.

"Hand me my bra, D'Eric. Thank you, boo." Tasia said taking the black lace bra from the toddler. D'Eric just smiled as he stared unblinkingly at the semi-nude female who wore nothing but a lime green thong. Her exposed caramel-complected breasts captivating the young boy.

"Tay! What the hell wrong *wit'* you?! Take your ass in the bathroom and get dressed! You be getting' dressed in front of my son!" Erica chastised. Her hands resting on her hips. D'Eric now stood with his tiny hands covering his eyes.

"Bitch, you *trippin'*. It ain't gonna hurt the boy to see some titties---you ain't raising no punk. Look, D'Eric, look." Tasia teased as she shook her miniature yet titillating breasts.

"That's what you call those, you flat-chested-ass hoe," Erica's snide remark made Tasia wince. She then walked into her own bedroom---knelt at the side of the bed and began groping beneath it, fondling shoe box after shoe box until he felt for the right one---Erica pulled out a Nike shoe box. Inside was rubber-banded stack of cash. About nineteen thousand dollars in cash.

She peeled sixteen crisp fifty-dollar bills from a stack. Then returned the shoe box to its hiding place. She was startled as she crammed the cash into her pocket---there stood Omarion. Erica had spent many hours just staring at Tasia's son, but now like all the other times the boy's face only revealed the features of his mother.

"Come here, Omarion." Erica beckoned. She picked up the toddler, held him high and examined his diaper closely. The waistband was emblazoned with pink teddy bears. "Tay! Tay! You diaper *thievin'* ass hoe!"

"What the fuck you *yellin'* about now?" Tasia asked dryly as she entered the bedroom.

"I'm yelling about you stealing my baby girl's diapers an' putting them on your lil' boy like dhat shit playa! Stop getting' your nails done and spend some money on your baby!"

Tasia snatched her son out of Erica's hands without saying another word.

**Chapter Three:**

Ball's arrogance was all the warmth he needed as he cruised down Green Street in his cocaine white 2015 Lexus IS 350 C, F-Sport, with its nineteen-inch Voss Gold Staggered rims glinting extraterrestrial like due to the LED wheel-well lighting. The nineteen-year-old dope boy was driving the 306-hp V6-bearing machine with the hardtop retracted in the forty-five-degree weather, Young Dolph's "Hold Up Hold Up Hold Up" blasting from the state-art sound system.

When he reached the intersection of Green Street and Maurice Street he yielded at the stop sign, turned up the volume and proceeded down Green St., his red plastic party cup in hand. The streetlights began to activate by timer as the evening sky became dusky.

Ball's one-carat diamond studs sparkled beneath his black fleece hoodie as he brought the Lexus to a slow crawl. A group of derriere-endowed, tightly clothed, color lace-front wig-wearing females paused in their strides, enthralled by Dolph's vocals.

"*Ballllllll!Ballllllll*! *Dat's* him!" the thick *yellow bone* in the white bodysuit and snake-skin ankle-cut boots yelled with adoration, her arms flailing excitedly. "Ball!"

Ball laughed to himself as he brought the automobile to a halt---he now had money and major status, which meant he had plenty of females on his dick. His beginnings had been meager---at sixteen he was birthed into the dope game with a sixteenth of an ounce, and as he grinded and saved, he watched as his cohorts rose and fell, became users of their supply, dodged, and got hit with prison sentence he remained. Flipping product and profit like a skilled gymnast until he had nonchalantly transformed from stone peddler to flamboyant brick mover.

He knew he was not handsome, not even attractive, but money had changed that---he maintained a fresh haircut and his dress code was narco-couture. And more importantly, he did not mind *tricking off* on a female. He had it, and they knew it.

A mocha-complected female in bright pink Moncler Ghany down vest and leggings snaked and gyrated her sensuous frame to the melodic sounds of Young Dolph. She was donning a tiny white tee despite the chill that went well with thigh-high boots.

"*Ooooh---dis* you?" LaLa asked ecstatically. Rubbing the ostrich-upholstered passenger seat sensually.

"Why would it not be? I don't fake or front," Ball proudly proclaimed. He was the rightful owner of Lexus. He had paid thirty-nine thousand dollars cash to the *'Migo* that ran the custom car shop in Camp Sutton, but the luxury vehicle was in his mother's name for tax purposes.

"Dat's what up!" LaLa's yellow thickness could hardly be contained by the Lycra fabric of her white bodysuit. Ball was liking what he was seeing. "You know my girls--- Alexis, Ciara, Deja'nee and Killa."

"Killa?" Ball's brow furled as the mocha-complected female waved daintily, continuing to sway to the music.

"Yeah, Killa---she's, my cousin. She moved here from Atlanta. She wok at Club Pleasers over by the McDonald's. Come here, Killa."

"Killa, dis Ball---remember, I was *tellin'* you about him, "LaLa stated to the female at her side. "Ball is major, one of the biggest dope boys in Monroe."

"Damn, you *doin'* it like *dhat?*" Killa asked, brushing a tree of two-tone colored hair from her face, revealing her wide violet contact-filled eyes.

"Somethin' like that," Ball answered modestly. "But I'm really *tryna* see how you do it up at that club.

"Big," Killa said seductively as she did a pirouette, with her backside to Ball she made her colossal ass clap. "Real, big daddy."

Ball was grinning from ear to ear. He looked over at the other three females---all three were curvaceous. One thing was certain, LaLa as fine as she was kept a flock of fine ass friends with her.

"You like dhat?" Killa asked before licking her lips.

"No doubt." His gaze intent. "What *ya'll* getting into."

"We was gonna go to the club. What you trying to get into?" LaLa asked as she continued to rub the ostrich upholstery, her breathing growing heavy.

"You already know."

LaLa looked at Killa who smiled and nodded---Killa kissed her on the lips and they both giggled.

"I thought ya'll was cousins."

"We is---*kissin'* cousins," LaLa said. Then she and Killa giggled.

LaLa's facial expression became serious. "Ball---you fucked anybody in dis car yet?" she asked looking unblinkingly in her eyes. He laughed, amazed at her bluntness.

"Nah, you tryna be first," Killa announced---her words coated with eroticism. Consuming the young hustler with her violet-colored eyes. The contacts gave her an exotic look. "You *feelin' dhat?*"

"No doubt. I'm feeling that. All ya'll *tryna* link up?" Ball looked over at the others gain, pointing with his cup of syrup---backs arched, hips flexed, and asses jolted out to tempt him further.

"You need to focus on us two---we goin' to fuck you good, daddy. Five of *us'll* fuck you to death," Killa purred, and they all burst into laughter. To Ball it sounded like a challenge, to the females it sounded as if he had a sexual death wish.

"Get in---everybody." Ball command coolly.

"Deja'nee, Alexis---Ciara! Ya'll come on," LaLa instructed as she quickly    got into the front seat. They scurried to the Lexus, clambering to the back seat.

"Ay! Yo---ya'll be easy on the interior. It's unbelievable as fuck--- I know. I know ya'll ain't seen *nothin'* like it befo'." Ball said as he turned the stereo up and took a sip of the syrup in his cup. Gucci Mane's "Stupid Wow' boomed from the speakers.

**Pipe It Up**

"I thought you said ya'll was gonna be here in a *lil'* bit, *sheiiiit*---I *coulda* went *wit'* Dana an' dem to hair shop if *I'da* knew this," Tasia's mother. Her hands on her hips.

Tasia's mother, Pam, was thirty-four years young, but had an even younger looking appearance and aura. She could have easily gone for twenty-three or twenty-four, easily. Her skin was the same succulent caramel as her daughter's, their height almost the same---their types totally different.

Pam was thickset, yet very curvaceous---her flawless face with its slanted eyes, button nose and luscious lips were coated with an unnecessary, but thin layer of makeup. Her hair was styled in a jet-black bob with platinum streaks and a flirtatious rat-tail. She wore a yellow form-fitting, velvet catsuit purchased from Shein with a pair of fuzzy yellow, Pink brand slippers.

"Why ya'll just now getting here, Tay?" Pam asked with irritation.

Tasia stood momentarily silent with Omarion in her arms, he was bundled in a toboggan and Gap fleece jacket." We took the kids to get *somethin'* to eat, momma---dang! If I don't feed your grandbaby before I bring him over you bitch," she explained curtly.

"You *ain't* been *feedin'* him, so I know you didn't have *nothin'* to do *wit'* it---that was Erica's doin'. Now move, so she can come in with them babies, an' hand me my grandbaby." Pam took Omarion into her arms, coddling and kissing him.

Tasia had not wanted to divulge too much information. They had fed the kids, but they had also used the opportunity as a disguise so that Erica could serve one of her steadfast customers---money and substantial amount of crack-cocaine had changed hands.

Erica staggered in with D'Eric clinging to her right leg and Nerica on her left hip, a small backpack in her hand.

"Oooh! Erica! I like yo' hair!" Pam exclaimed, shuffling over to get a better look at her funky hairstyle.

"I like yours," Erica replied as Nerica struggled to break free and go to Pam. Pam gladly accepted the child into her arm.

"Hey, baby---you miss Auntie Pam?" Nerica nodded, her hand in her smiling mouth.

Pam immediately noticed the backpack in Erica's hand. "Tay, did you bring any diapers or clothes for Omarion?" She asked sternly.

"No, 'cause we goin' to come get 'em in the morning."

"Why you can't be more like Erica, she brought diapers and clothes for her kids.

"Actually---Ms. Pam, I brought somethin'---Tay sorry-ass don't never bring shit. She don't care if the boy eat or walk around *wit'* shit on 'em."

Tasia looked at Erica with resentment then rolled her eyes and smacked her lips loudly.

"Look, momma---we'll be by in the *mornin'* to pick the babies up," Tasia stated, trying to change the subject.

"Hold up, Tay---what about the money! I ain't even got my check cashed yet---damn!"

"Where you gonna get the check cashed anyway? It's after six now!"

"Mangum's, they don't close until seven-thirty on Fridays," Tasia answered matter-of-factly.

"You can't bring me my piece of money back after you leave Mangum's---I told Travis I'd let him hold somethin'!!"

"Momma! I ain't givin' you no money so you can give it away--- and Travis!! Momma you still messing wit' that *boy?* They gon' lock yo' ass up!" Tasia scolded.

"You *ain't givin'* me shit! You returning money you owe me--- what the fuck wrong with yo' silly ass? And I'm a grown ass woman, don't nobody tell me who to give this pussy to--- look at you? You got me *cussin' an' talkin'* nasty in front of these babies," Pam explained as she shook her head and placed Omarion and Nerica on the floor---they calmly walked to the couch in front of the television, D'Eric followed.

"Momma, you old enough to be that boy's momma---he a year younger than me!"

"Yeah, but he eats pussy like he thirty-eight." Pam chuckled, extending her hand to Erica for a high-five.

"That's right, Ms. Pam. Get yours," Erica encouraged with a laugh.

"Let's go, Erica." Tasia insisted.  "Let's go---Momma, I'll bring you your money in the mornin' when we come and get the kids."

Erica peeled a fifty-dollar bill from her bankroll---handed it to Pam, then she and Tasia left. Tasia was fuming from the act of generosity.

## PART II: YELLOW LIGHT

Yellow lights provide a cautionary warning to indicate that you should slow down.

*SLOOOOOOOOOW DOOOOOOOOWN!*

## Chapter Four: BALL

Twista and R. Kelly's "Yellow Light" exuded from the speakers dampening everyone in the motel room with sensuousness---all eyes were on Killa as she stood on the dresser oscillating her mocha-complected, white thong-covered ass. Her fuchsia and black mohawk damp with perspiration. Hands went to knees as she wobbled and *p-popped*.

Ball and LaLa sat on the massive bed sharing a cup of syrup watching the striptease intently--- when Ball pulled out a baggie of cocaine and tossed it on the nightstand the other females fought over it like Pitbull pups fighting over the last remaining teat.

Ball found it truly hard to get comfortable, especially with his intestines feeling like knotted ropes---the laxative he had taken only complicating the matter. The continuous consumption of the codeine-promethazine cocktails had him constipated.

"Un-uh---Ciara, you go last *wit' dem* big ass nostril," Dejanee announced with urgency. Her mahogany skin perspiring.

"Fuck you, bitch!"

"Ay, ya'll be easy," Ball said with a grimace as he stood and headed towards the bathroom. "When I come *outta* the bathroom I wanna see what that's about." He was pointing at Killa's plump ass."

"And why do they call you Killa anyway?" Ball asked, standing in the doorway of the bathroom.

"Because this pussy I got is Killa, daddy." She laughed and wiggled. "Why they call you Ball?"

"Cause that's what I do--- you see the car, the VVS diamonds, the clothes." Ball was fitted in a black Nike Tech fleece hoodie, black Nike joggers and a pair of black Vapor Max sneakers with metallic and day-glow green accents.

He quickly disappeared into the bathroom, locked the door, dropped his joggers to his ankles and straddled the porcelain toilet. He rocked, strained, grunted and pushed---nothing. Nothing would escape his bowels and it had been that way for the past three days. The about of constipation beating down the euphoric sensation that once consumed his body. He wanted another cup of purple panacea, he needed it.

Ball sat on the toilet so long his legs had fallen asleep.

"Ball! *Balllllll!* You *ain't* dead in *dhere* is you?" LaLa asked with loud nervousness. But Ball did not hear that---her question had come out *chopped* and *screwed*. He could not see her, but he imagined the words dripping slowly from her mouth like water from a faucet.

"I'm *a'ight*," he groaned.

"You sure?"

"*Yeahhhhh.*"

LaLa walked away from the bathroom door giggling, her hand covering her mouth. Killa came down off the dresser and moved to the bed, quickly scooping up the keys to Ball's Lexus. "Let's go ya'll." Her tone low.

"Where we going?" Alexis asked in a whisper.

"Wherever we *wanna* go---*ol'* boy left his keys out here an' he been in there damn near an hour---let's go LaLa."

LaLa and the other girls gathered their things. "Killa, what about yo' pants and yo' boots? You ain't got on no pants," LaLa announced.

"We *comin'* back---besides I wanna feel **dhat** ostrich interior against my ass," Killa explained. They all laughed as they tiptoed furtively out of the motel room and to the car.

## CHAPTER FIVE: THAT'S MESSED UP

"Yo! Look! They out there towing your boy shit! There go one of his partners out there---no two of 'em," Corey informed everyone as he continued watching the tow truck operator do his job.

"*Dhat* nigga gonna be pissed when he findout he ain't got no stereo system or rims," Axe chuckled as he worked the game controller compulsively in his hands---the computerized Chad Johnson zig-zagged into the end zone. He then passed the blunt to Sleepy.

"Fuck the blunt, pass the controller---I'm *tryin'* to get my Madden on, too." Sleepy complained before taking a toke of the *piff*. "Don't even worry 'bout it. Why ya'll playin' in some pussy."

Axe's brow raised. Corey scratched under his arm, unable to comprehend. Man ignored the frivolous talk and worked his controller diligently while Axe was not paying attention.

"Who pussy you think you getting ready to be *playin'* in?" Axe asked.

"Tay." Sleepy said matter-of-factly as he passed the blunt to Corey.

"Freaky-ass Tay?"

"Yeah, I'm *s'posed* to meet her at Club Blackout."

"Ain't her and Eric livin' together?" Axe quizzed.

"Yeah---in the Third Drive."

"What happened to what we talked about? You done fell in love or somethin'?"

"Fuck you nigga! I don't fall in love. That shit for *suckas*!" Sleepy was frustrated---his pretty face now contorted into a grimace.

"So, what's up?" Axe was growing heated, feeling that his partner-in-crime was making an indirect attack on his relationship with Tashay. "Erica *movin' dhat* work---she *fuckin' wit'* that Mexican, so I know she sitting on at least a brick. If she *holdin'* for her man, she probably *sittin'* on three or *fou'* bricks! Plus, dhat paper!"

Axe was now animated---the wheels in his head turning and churning as he contemplated how much cocaine and money two defenseless, young women could possibly have in their possession.

"So---what's up?!"

"I'm wit' it, but we need to hold up---let me see what's *poppin'* first. I know Tay be tryna do her *thang*, too. So, we want 'em both to be holding, make sure we come off," Sleep explained.

***********************************************

No one could tell Tasia she was not the shit, at least not tonight. She had her check cashed, hair done, nails done, a new outfit and she was as high as a hot-air balloon.

The deejay was spinning SZA's "I Hate You" and the females in the club were definitely *moving it* in a room full vultures---Tasia was sandwiched between two ruffians who grinded against her suggestively as she sang along with the songstress. Her eyes closed as she sang along drunkenly and passionately. The taller of the two attempted to ease his hand down the crotch of her jeans. Erica watched it all from the bar as she nursed a drink an admirer had ordered for her.

"Ay! Nigga!" Sleepy blurted as he pulled at the ruffian's arm aggressively. "I *'on't* give a fuck about no tough looks. Fall back!"

Both ruffians backed away from Tasia saying nothing but continuing to shoot deathly stares at Sleepy. "Why you *trippin'*? We was just dancing! *Dang!*" Tasia exclaimed.

Sleepy really and truly did not care who Tasia danced with, who stuck their hands down her jeans or who she had sex with, but he had to make her believe he was *feeling* her. Especially, if he planned to stick her and her friend for their *paper*.

"I thought you was gonna let me beat tonight," Sleepy said giving her a straight face that was oh-so seductive. Tasia felt herself growing moist---those dreamy, bedroom eyes the hoodlum possessed did that to her. As did the street jargon in which he spoke.

Tasia threw her arms around his sinewy, yet slender shoulders. "*I'mma* let you *beat*, Barron. Stop trippin'," she purred in his ear.

"What I tell you 'bout that?" Sleepy asked harshly as he gripped her petite ass in his hands.

"Okay---Sleepy." She giggled as she inhaled his scent---a combination of marijuana smoke and Creed Aventus cologne. She loved teasing him about his name, loved how it provoked him.

Tasia looked over at Erica who was now being wooed by a Dior-clad hustler who was wearing ultra-dark Dior aviator sunglasses. Envy filled Tasia's core as she watched the hustler lean into Erica and whisper into her ear---she pondered what it was about her friend that had all the *d-boys* and hustlers interested.

*So what? She hustles a little crack and weed---and don't rely on a man to pay her bills---they can't be looking to wife her? She got two kids by different men and she always up in the club. They can't be, can they?* Tasia's thoughts had her biting her bottom lip.

"*I'mma* go see if Erica ready to go." Tasia announced. Aware of the fact that Sleepy did not have a car.

"Why we gotta wait?"

"Huh?!" Tasia had a look of bewilderment on her face.

"I said, why we gotta wait?" Sleepy bore a seduce smirk on his brown face. His drowsy eyes enticing.

*Damn! Them eyes!* Tasia mentally screamed.

"What you talkin' 'bout, Sleepy?"

"I'm talking about us *slidin'* to the bathroom so I can *beat that*."

She was tempted but thought about the filthiness of the club's bathroom. "I ain't sliding to no bathroom *wit'* you---let's just wait 'til we get to Erica's. Okay?" She purred as she stroked his smooth face.

"That's what's up," Sleepy said with disappointment in his tone. It was theatrics.

"Don't act like that. I'ma give you the *bidness*, I promise." And with that said Tasia walked over to Erica as Duke Deuce's "Crunk Ain't Dead" blared throughout the club.

"Girl let's roll to the crib," Tasia suggested. Interrupting her friend's conversation. Erica rolled her eyes.

"Tay---don't you see I'm *talkin'*? Rude-ass bitch!"

"Bring him with you.' Tasia said looking over Erica's shoulder to the hustler she was conversing with. He smiled, appreciating the assistance.

"Mind your fuckin' business!' Erica scolded. "That lil' droopy eyed fake-ass thug of yours done showed up, now you ready to go!"

The patrons inside the club became rowdier as the deejay teased them, scratching and mixing in the HoneyKomb Brazy's street track "Yellow."

"*I'ma* be real with you---I don't want that nigga in my house! He probably got warrants! He robbed somebody today---him an' Axe. He grimy as fuck, Tay!"

"Don't do that, Erica." Tasia looked at her friend with pleading eyes. "Sleepy good people. You know Axe have him doin' stupid shit--- come on, Erica!"

"A'ight, but the first time he get to acting stupid---I want his ass out my house."

"Okay. I got you."

"I'm serious, Tay."

"Okay!" Tay answered. Smiling uncomfortably as she walked away.

Erica looked at the go-getter who had been trying to persuade her to go to a hotel with him for the past forty minutes and smiled. "You wanna go home with me?" She asked, but it was a rhetorical question. He licked his lips as he basked in his small victory. He still had to get into her panties.

"What you think?" He asked with a smile. Erica took him by the hand and led him towards Tasia and Sleepy. He froze---eyes wide with imminent fear. "That's the dude ya'll was talkin' about?"

"Yeah, why? What's up?" Erica frowned.

"Nah, shorty---I'ma have to get with you some other time," he muttered as he backed away.

Erica looked at both Sleepy and Tasia with disdain. If looks could kill the couple would have been dead from the look Erica was giving them.

"Where your lil' *entanglement* going?" Tasia asked.

"The hell away from your grimy-ass bed-buddy!" Erica's tone was dry.

"Come on now! Don't do that! I *'on't* even know that man," Sleepy pleaded. Even in the dimly lit club Erica could see how a woman could get lost in his bedroom eyes.

Erica quickly surveyed the club for an *ole reliable*---a lover from her past that could satisfy her sexual appetite just for tonight. She spotted a few familiar faces, but they were the faces of those who could not last beyond five minutes or **homeless-sexuals**,

"*Kennnnnnny*!" Erica yelled across the crowded club; desperation tinged her voice. He was in heavy conversation with what appeared to be a duo of significantly loud Charlotte natives partaking in Monroe mischief. Typical "704 shit" ---libation, marijuana smoking and drug talk.

Kenny craned his neck her direction, lowering his sunglasses so that his eyes could focus. In doing so he revealed that his right eye had been blackened---it was too late, he had spotted Erica and she had spotted his eye.

"Shit," she muttered. She had to commit to the cause. She had an itch, and she knew Kenny could scratch it. Erica could see him coming towards her, his sunglasses again concealing his eyes.

Kenny Dobbs---better known as Pretty Kenny was a lothario in the worst way. At just twenty-two years old, the light-skinned, muscular built hoodlum had mastered the art of pleasing women sexually, so much so that his *sex game* affected them mentally. When a woman did not give herself to him freely, he stole from her---stole her sexual soul. Disappeared for days, then returned just when her body yearned to be pleased again---his wrongs forgotten and his pleasure in demand.

Kenny, too, like Erica was from Maurice Street Projects---now known as Grace Gardens, and he had bedded almost every woman who was not of senior citizen status and every young girl that he could without it being classified a pedophile. Sexually slaying practically every available female from Grace Gardens' First Drive to its Fourth Drive.

"What's good, baby?" Kenny's melodic tone embraced her before his massive arms did. Erica's thick frame almost went limp in his arms. "Damn, you smell good!"

"Thank you," she answered as she gathered herself. "What happened to your eye?"

Erica was blunt.

"Uh, I---got into a little scuffle," he replied. His sunglasses concealing his eyes, which were looking off to the left to avoid the topic.

"Wit' who?"

"Turtle," he mumbled as he stroked her arms.

"Turtle?! Turtle! What you fighting *wit'* Turtle for?" Erica stood back, hands on her hips, her weight resting on her hind positioned leg. She frowned as she pondered the reasons for Kenny and Turtle engaging in a physical confrontation---she remembered what Theresa had told her. Mary Anne had been talking to someone in a burgundy car. Kenny had a burgundy car.

Kenny scratched his head, his naturally curly hair shifting beneath his fingers. 'What was you *screamin'* at me across the club for?" Attempting to change the subject.

"Because." Erica answered. Pretending to be shy---her knees together as she swayed from side to side.

"'Cause what?" Kenny teased as he cupped her chin in his hand and gave her that sensual smile that he owned and utilized every chance he got.

"Because---I'm *finna* go home and I want you to go home with me," she said with seductive conviction.

"Meet me in the parking lot. I bought my car so I'mma follow you. I just gotta holla at somebody real quick."

They quickly parted ways. Kenny heading for the door.

## CHAPTER SIX

"I knew we *shouldna* took his car---look at dat shit! Ball *gon'* kill us!" LaLa yelled as she examined the dented bumper and fractured taillight of the Lexus.

"Us?! Us---I didn't even wanna leave the room, but I did because ya'll my bitches! And I'ma do whatever ya'll do---but I'm not *wearin'* this!" Alexis ranted.

"Didn't nobody make you get in, ain't nobody put a gun to your big ass heads!" Dejanee argued.

"*Damnnnnn!* Ay, Sexy---what you *doin'* out here *wit'* no clothes on?" The shifty-looking hooligan in a black Ralph Lauren puffer jacket and black Timberland boots. "You tryin' to get fucked?"

His gold-toothed associate grinned sinisterly.

Killa stood shivering, her white thong exposed and illuminated by the LED lighting in the car's wheel-well. She folded her arms across her breasts, hiding what her tee could not. Her face contorted as she rolled her eyes at the hooligans.

"Here, girl--- *'fore* you get raped!" Alexis exclaimed as she removed her jacket and tossed it to her friend. Killa put the jacket on then hopped in place for warmth---the ruffians ogling at her jiggling ass.

"Oh! Shit! Dat's Killa from Club Pleasers!" The gold-toothed hooligan exclaimed as he grabbed his crotch. Being recognized as a ghetto superstar forced Killa to react as one---foolish. She lifted the jacket and began making her derriere clap. "Ay! Killa! We 'bout to get a room, what you and your girls tryin' to get into?"

"We already got a room. We at the Motel 6." She answered, pointing in no particular direction.

"Don't tell them where we staying!" Ciara blurted.

"Let's go! Killa get yo' stupid ass in the car!" LaLa demanded. "I'm *drivin'!* and ya'll need to come up *wit'* something to tell Ball before we get back to the room."

"No, Killa need to be coming up with something, she the one backed into that pole on some stripper shit," Ciara said matter-of-factly as they piled into the luxury vehicle.

**************************************************************************
*

## BALL OF FIRE

Ball pulled up his jeans as he stood. A bit of expelled gas barely easing the abdominal pain brought on by his constipation. "Ya'll quiet as fuck in here," he said as he exited the bathroom. The room itself was empty---no potential sex partners anywhere. Abruptly his bowels churned, and he closed the door, swiftly dropped his pants and sat back on the towel bowl. He swore to himself that he was done drinking *syrup-*--Actavis Promethazine Phosphate cough syrup.

"*Uuunnnhhhhh!*" He groaned as he doubled over, his head between his knees. Ball swore to himself that he was done drinking **lean**.

## CHAPTER SEVEN

Back at Erica's apartment sex and Peanut Butter Breath cannabis was in the air and the sounds of lovemaking were being masked by the rhythm and blues that escaped from the stereo that played loudly in the living room. In the children's room Sleepy lay back on the bed with his eyes closed while Tasia did what she did best---gave the lanky, naked body a tongue-bath.

Sleepy was impatient, he pushed Tasia's head from his thigh to his manhood. She swallowed his dick like a professional, regurgitated it, then swallowed it again---regurgitated, swallowed, then teased the tip with her tongue.

Inside Eric's bedroom they had long been finished with the foreplay. Kenny stood behind Erica with one foot propped on the bed to strengthen his stroke---Erica was on her hands and knees with her big legs spread and her dark chocolate ass positioned at the edge of the bed. Giving her lover full access to pound her pussy from the back.

"Who---pussy---dis?! Who--- pussy---dis?!" Kenny grunted with each thrust. Their flesh smacking together.

"It's yours," she purred as she dug her fingernails into the bedsheets. "It's *youuuuurs*, Kenny! Oooh, *sheeeeit*!"

Erica's praise excited Kenny and he thrusted harder---faster. One hand on her shoulder, the other on her hip, pulling her further onto his stiff dick.

************************************************************

Axe walked out of the bedroom rubbing his baldhead. "Ay! Ya'll gotta get the fuck outta here! My girl tryna sleep---straight up," he vented.

"A'ight, Axe. Chill! One more game and then we gone. I gotta get some of my money back," Corey explained. Preparing to play Man in a fifth game of BCFX on Xbox. Man's NCCU defense had shutdown Corey's Clark Atlanta team for four straight games.

For the last five minutes Clark Atlanta's drumline had been *putting on for the city* and it sounded as if they were in the living room performing live. Which had Tashay in the bedroom angry and unwilling to make a sexual compromise---and Axe wanted some pussy.

"Nigga, did you hear what the fuck I said?! Get the fuck up out my crib!" Axe yelled. Standing over Corey shirtless, wearing flimsy grey sweatpants, his pecs flexing.

Man stood and moved towards the door without a word---not because he was scared. He was always quiet, and it was late. He was tired.

"Man---where you goin'? Axe *bullshittin'*," Corey said as he reset the game. Axe turned the television off.

"Nigga, I ain't playin'! Get the fuck out!" Axe roared.

**********************************************************
**

"Oh! *Gawwwd!* I'm comin'! I'm comin', Kenny! I'm---*ummm, gawwwd!* I'm *commmin'!* I'm *com-innn'!*" Erica screamed as Kenny continued doing what he did best---delivering pleasurable pain.

Erica was climaxing for the third time. Her thick frame was wet and warm, perspiration dripping off her nipples and between the crevice of her ass cheeks. Kenny, himself had built up a sweat.

She looked back over her shoulder to watch Kenny work---a focused look in his eyes as he long-stroked her womanhood. She unconsciously bit into her bottom lip and moaned as she eyed his taut muscles. Even his blackened eye was now sexy. "*Ahhh!* Right there, Kenny!" She cried out.

Kenny pumped and thrusted as if he was dancing to a Reggae tune---his dick slapping every nerve-ending inside Erica's hot, wet pussy.

Inside the children's room Tasia rode Sleepy's dick like a seizing nymphomaniac. As uncomfortable as it was Sleepy continued to allow her to bounce and grind clumsily on his shaft. Tasia had already sucked the life out of him---he knew she was trying to get *hers* by any means.

Sleepy was determined to deal with a little dick-chafing if the result meant he would learn where the money and dope was stashed.

"Yes! Yes! *Mmm-mhh*! I'm coming!" Tasia blurted, her back arched and her eyes closed. Sleepy reached up and gently squeezed her same hot, wet mouth that had consumed his semen just fifteen minutes earlier.

*********************************************************
***

Just as LaLa, Killa, Dejanee, Alexis and Ciara were tiptoeing back into the hotel room, Ball was exiting the bathroom for a third time---his features seeming a little bit more relaxed than earlier.

"Hey, Daddy," Killa purred with excitement as she rushed into Ball's arms. "*Lissen*---I knew you heard the noise, but it's not as bad as it sounded. Some *muthaphukka musta* been drunk, hit yo' shit an' kept going."

"Heard what noise? I ain't hear shit! Hit who shit?!" Ball exclaimed as he tried to wrestle free from Killa's intertwining embrace. Killa continued with her fictious explanation.

"Somebody hit yo' car---by the time we got outside whoever did it was gone. It was nothing major though."

"She's right, Ball. It's nothing major." LaLa attempted to reassure him as Dejanee and Ciara shook their heads in agreement. Alexis remained expressionless.

Ball stamped out of the room to where his Lexus was parked, everyone followed behind him. He inspected the front of the car---found no damage. It was his inspection of the vehicle's rear that set off his rage. "*Awwwh! Naaaww!* What the fuck?! *Naaaw,* man!" Ball yelled as he paced the parking lot.

"How ya'll let somebody hit my shit," he continued. "Didn't none of ya'll see who it was? The car?! *Anythaaang?!*"

"We was in the room, just like you," LaLa explained. "We heard it, then ran out here. You know if we seen who did it, we would tell you."

"You know we'd tell you, Ball." Ciara insisted. "We fuck with you."

Ball for the first time was looking at Ciara's face---not her ample derriere, but her face. Ciara's skin was the color of rosewood. Her dark brown eyes were mysterious and her dimpled-cheeks innocent.

Killa approached him from behind and brought her hands under his arms, up to his chest which she caressed as she rested her head against his back. "Don't trip, daddy. Let's go back in the room and I promise we'll take your mind off this situation---okay?" She suggested as she nudged him towards the motel room entrance.

"We got you," LaLa said with a seductive smirk on her yellow-complected face. "And me an' you still gon' fuck in your car."


**************************************************
**


Tasia was sound asleep in the bedroom which gave Sleepy the perfect opportunity to snoop around---he rambled through kitchen cabinets and drawers in the dark as quietly as he could, having found nothing in the children's room or bathroom. Nothing but a bottle of penicillin pills. The prescription label bore Tasia's name and had been prescribed over a month ago. That had brought on a sigh of relief.

Sleepy opened a drawer which contained Erica's digital scales---he quickly pushed one of the scales into his pants pocket. Then continue snooping. He found no drugs or money, but he noticed a medium sized pot, a glass jar and large spoon in the dry-rack next to the sink. He knew what it meant---a *re-up* had been completed.

Sleepy smiled, but only for a moment---he was startled and blinded by the light.

"What the fuck you *doin' ramblin'* in my kitchen?" Erica uttered. She stood in a tight-fitting tank tee and hi-cut panties, her hands on her hips. Sleepy turned around speechless. "Can you hear? What you doin' in my kitchen?"

"Uh-uh, I'm---uh, lookin' for somethin' to eat," Sleepy tried to explain as he stared at her broad hips and the alluring print of her pussy which was very visible through the sheer yellow fabric. Her dark chocolate breasts like large coconuts practically spilling out of her tank-tee with each enraged breath.

"You *shoulda* ate *befo'* you came over here. This *ain't* no soup kitchen."

"Hold up, Erica---why you always comin' at my neck? We used to be cool," Sleepy stated as he composed himself. He stepped towards her, so close that she could feel the heat that exuded from his bare, tattooed chest.

"You right, Sleepy---we did used to be cool, but you know what happened? You started runnin' with that fool Axe! Doin' the same stupid shit he be doin'---you gonna end up in prison just like---"

"Nathan," Sleepy interjected before she could get it out.

"Yeah, like Nathan."

Their eyes met; they held each other's gaze as the seconds passed. Then their gazes dropped---Sleepy's to Erica's womanhood. While Erica's gaze slowly trailed down his chiseled chest and abs to bulge in his jeans. Her gaze shot back up to his eyes---sexy, bedroom eyes. She licked her bottom lip as temptation warmed her.

Sleepy leaned in, his lips bound for her neck. "Uhn-un! What you think you doin', Sleepy? You fuck wit' my best girl. You know I don't rock like that. *Sor-ry,*" Erica said dryly.

He put his hands on her waist and backed her into the stove. "Don't be like that, this me," he pleaded. Erica was stuck between the stove and Sleepy's hard place.

"That's why it's not going down, because it's you---so that's the only way I can be."

"Erica---Erica?" Sleepy looked at her with a look of longing.

"*Uhn-unn*, don't look at me like that. It's not goin' down," she insisted. Feeling herself become vulnerable. Sleepy's fingertips teased her rich, chocolatey thighs, sending a tingle throughout her body.

"Look---it ain't gonna happen, so back there where your girl is, let her deal with that," Erica said patting his bulging crotch. "Or get out my house 'cause you ain't gon' be creeping around this *muthaphukka* like it's cool."

*************************************************************
***

Killa was naked and straddled atop Ball's lap in a reverse-cowgirl position, rocking and rolling her big ass. Looking at herself in the mirror directly across from the bed while Ciara, Alexis and Dejanee were sprawled across the adjacent bed watching videos. Every so often Ciara snuck a peek at the uninhibited sex act. LaLa stood at the sink trying to stop her cocaine-induced nosebleed.

Ball felt like a boss. He had a roomful of thoroughbreds who were willing to suck semen from a dog's dick if he showed them enough money and coke. And now he had the finest of the five gyrating on his shaft with slow precision. Providing him with a sensual view of her backside as she worked her lower half, her hands on his shins for balance and support.

Ball looked over at LaLa who was now reapplying her makeup. She was geeked up on the high-grade cocaine and he knew she would do whatever he asked once he was finished with Killa. Maybe he would have them fuck each other--- the thought had crossed his devious mind.

At that time the door splintered open with a thunderous boom. "*Er'body* lay the fuck down!" The gunman brandishing the *humongous serpent* commanded. The Romanian-built Draco with a 30-round magazine commanded the crowd's attention like an upset grade schoolteacher. His partner who pointed a .38 revolver said nothing as he entered, but it did not take Killa or any of the other females long to recognize the two *jack boys*.

"Get the fuck down!" the once silent hooligan shouted as he gun-butted a stupefied LaLa with the burl wood handle on the weapon. She screamed as she collapses to the floor like a feeble box.

Ball just lay on the bed frightened, naked and with a limp dick. The trail of hickeys from his neck to his navel looked more like sores now that fear had constricted his blood vessels---stopping the blood flow.

Dejanee cried tears of anger---she knew if it had not been for Killa's loose lips they would not be looking down the barrels of guns.

"Where it at, nigga?" The gold-tooth hooligan rushed over to Ball and put the gun to his temple.

"Where what? I -I ain't g-got nothin'," Ball stammered. The *jackboy* jammed the gun into Ball's eye socket causing him lose control of his bladder. "Man, I ain't got nothing but a couple stacks! I-I swear to *Gaawd!* Man! But you can get it! Just don't kill me, man!"

"Shut up, nigga! *Dhese* bitches *ain't* crying as much as *yo'* pussy-ass," the hooligan said easing the gun from Ball's face. Ball's eyes met Ciara's and he instantly felt ashamed of his own cowardice.

"Please don't kill me! Ya'll can have the money---I ain;t tryna die for this shit," he continued to plead and beg.

Killa looked up from the floor at Ball. She knew it was her fault they were in such a deathly situation, but she could not help but notice that Ball was bawling like a bitch. Every tear that trickled from his eyes she lost a dram of respect for the young dope boy.

"Shut the fuck up!" The revolver-wielding *jackboy* shouted, disgusted with Ball. "*Whereitaaaat?!*"

"It's—it's—it's in my shoes," he whimpered.

"In *yo'* shoes?!" The hoodlums blurted in unison. The gold-toothed hooligan recognized Ball's method for what it was and made a conscious decision to expose him. "Oh, you slick nigga! You put your money in your shoe because you thought one of these hoes was *gon'* try and get you. You *ain't* got to worry about that now."


The *jackboys* laughed as they aggressively pulled stacks of cash from the insides of the trapper's sneakers, plucking the laces from the eyelets as they greedily snatched the money. Then the least vocal of the two grabbed Ball's jeans from the floor and riffled through the pockets. "We got *dat clean*," he announced with a smile. Holding in his palm a baggie that contained a little less than fourteen grams of cocaine.

"Let's go!" And without another word the hooligans backpedaled out of the room. The night air rushed in from the open door, more frigid than before---chilling the bare flesh of everyone.

The semi-hysterical females scrambled from the floor and began to recant the happenings from only a few seconds ago while Ball nervously fought to get his legs into his jeans simultaneously.

As quickly as it had happened the first time, it happened a second time---the two *jackboys* invaded the motel room. "I forgot to give you somethin', nigga," the gold-toothed gunman explained. *"I'on't* want you *thinkin'* shit sweet. You might get some heart and come at us."

***Baawwhh! Baawwhh!!!*** Two hollow-point rounds caught Ball in the thigh and stomach. Ciara, Dejanee and Killa screamed, but no one could hear them, they could not even hear themselves---not with the prominent ringing in their ears. No one saw the jackboys leave, but they had---swiftly.

LaLa and Alexis were huddled in the corner crying hysterically, oblivious to the absence of the *jackboys*.

************************************************************
****

Erica waddled into the kitchen barefoot wearing nothing but baby blue panties and a head scarf. Despite the hot shower a pleasurable soreness still taunted her midsection and inner thighs. Tasia was standing at the stove scrambling eggs. "Girl, Kenny put it on my ass last night," Erica blurted. Embarrassed once she noticed Sleepy sitting at the kitchen table. Not because of the information she'd revealed, but because of what she was revealing---herself. She was damn-near naked, and relaxed. Her belly seeming pouchlike. "What the fuck is he still doin' in my house? It's goin' on two o'clock!"

'Oh, uh---Tay *fixin'* me *somethin'* to eat," Sleepy explained, sitting at the table in nothing but his socks and boxers.

"Who the fuck talkin' to you? I'm talking to Tay! Tay! Why is he still here?"

"We ain't too long woke up. Damn! I told him I'd fix him something to eat before he go," Tasia said dryly as she scraped the eggs from the pan onto the plate. "Why is you trippin'?"

"What's the rule. Tay? What's the rule?" Erica yelled. The veins in her neck like cordage. Sleepy stared at her hungrily as her large breasts heaved.

Tasia rolled her eyes and exhaled loudly. "Overnight company must be gone by one in the morning," she mumbled, scratching her thong-covered ass as she placed the plate on the table. Avoiding Erica's intimidating gaze.

"Tay! Tay!"

"What?" She exclaimed as she looked at Erica with a sexual.

"If you want me to leave, Erica, just say so." Sleepy uttered.

"Who the fuck talkin' to you?! But since you insist on being a part of this conversation---yeah, I want you to leave. You gotta go!" Erica said curtly. Her arms folded across her bare breasts.

"Ay, Tay---throw eggs on some bread for me," Sleepy said as he got up from the table and walked towards the bedroom.

"I told you last night that this wasn't no soup kitchen," Erica continued. "Tay, you my girl an' all---but you wearing out your welcome real quick---too quick. When your lil' company leaves we gotta talk, then I *gotta* handle *somethin'* important."

Sleepy returned to the kitchen fully dressed---he grabbed the egg sandwich, kissed Tasia on the cheek and smacked her on the ass. She giggled, punching him playfully in the arm. "I'ma holla at you later, a'ight?" He said as he moved towards the backdoor slowly.

"Sleepy," Tasia purred with seductiveness. He turned, giving her his attention. "You better get at me later. I'm for real."

Sleepy took all of her in as she stood there in her boy-beater and thong, her hands clasped in front of her, concealing her special place. A place he had prodded and probed for most of the early part of the morning. "I'ma holla," he said reassuringly as he accepted his egg sandwich. "Bye, Erica."

"Whatever, nigga."

*********************************************************************

It was 7:18p.m.--- LaLa and Ciara sat quietly inside Ball's hospital room. While Killa smacked loudly, devouring his dinner tray---tuna salad, seasoned green beans, banana pudding and a cup of orange juice. Dejanee and Alexis had gone home hours ago. No one in the room had changed or showered and the stench of alcohol, drugs and sex exuded from their pores.

"This all your fault---none of this *woulda* happen if you'd kept your mouth shut," Ciara whispered as the heart monitor beeped at a steady pace. Indicating that Ball was among the living. "You had to tell them hoods what motel we were at. I *shouldna* let you take Ball's car--- that's what really brought all this on in the first place."

"Bitch, will you shut the hell up. I'm so sick of yo' fuckin' mouth." Killa's monotone was dry and vulgar.

"Ya'll need to keep it down, ya'll see he tryna sleep," LaLa interjected in a low tone.

"Tryin' to sleep?! He doped the fuck up. He got shot the fuck up. I could shoot a gun in this bitch---he wouldn't *wake up!!*" Killa blurted with disregard.

"The way you *smackin'* over there you sound like a little twenty-five, any-way! Pop. Pop. Pop. Close your mouth you no home-*trainin' havin' biiiitch!*" Ciara was fuming as the nurse entered.

"Excuse me---you girls do know this is a hospital, don't you?" The ill-tempered, middle-aged, white nurse asked. Her pink scrubs emblazoned with flowers.

"No shit." Killa said rudely before gulping down a spoonful of banana pudding.

"No shit," the nurse mocked, her hands on her hips. "It's not a food bank either. You've got an EBT card, use it. Don't be eating this poor soul's dinner."

"You got a jazzy-ass mouth on you old lady." The girls snickered.

Killa and the nurse went back and forth with the snide remarks for a full ten minutes before LaLa and Ciara calmed them down.

"You girls have to leave," the nurse announced in a placid tone.

"Leave! Leave for what?" LaLa exclaimed. Her white bodysuit bore brown smudges, stained with Ball's dried blood. The lump on her forehead from being butted with a gun had decreased substantially.

"I've already *let* you stay past the designated visitation time. Now it's not up for discussion---you girls have gotta leave."

"Let, *unnh*---let 'em stay for a few more minutes." Ball croaked as his eyes came open.

"Well, look at you. You're finally awake," the nurse continued to speak in a placid tone. "Are you hungry?"

She gave Killa an evil-eyed glance.

"Nah, but I'm *kinda* thirsty."

"I'll be back in a sec'. how does apple juice sound?"

"That's cool." Ball winced with pain. The nurse left the room.

"How you feelin'?" LaLa was the first to ask she sidled up to the hospital bed and began rubbing the wounded trapper's arm.

"Like shit," he grumbled looking from face to face. When he saw Ciara, he dropped his gaze and shame consumed his injured frame.

"Ball, they had guns. There was nothin' you could do---I'm sure if you would've had a gun, you'd have busted it," Ciara said with strong reassurance and sympathy. Gazing at the shell of the young hustler. Ball refused to give her eye contact.

Killa rolled her violet-colored eyes, pushed the bed tray away and sauntered over to his bedside. *Why don't you tell her that if you'd had a gun you woulda probably shot yourself in your pussy little dick with it---* she thought as she looked at Ball, putting on a fake smile. "You okay, daddy?" She asked.

Ball grunted as a response. Killa stroked his face gently. He grunted again---this time it was due to the discomfort of the catheter lodged in his dick. Killa could arouse even the wounded and bedridden.

All the females focused on the protrusion in the center of the university blue blanket and smirked. "You want some don't *'cha*?" Killa teased.

"What you think?" Ball's remark was rhetorical as he, himself, focused on the protrusion.

"I think you need to hurry up an' get out of the hospital, so you can get the Lexus fixed and I can fuck you in it *wit'* the top down," she purred in his ear.

"*Unh*-uh---Ball know what time it is. Tell her, ain't nothin' goin' down unless my juicy ass in that Lexus, too." LaLa interjected as she leaned in, her full lips brushing against Ball's cheek. But he was preoccupied.

"Ay, uh---where my Lex at?"

"Oh! It's in the parking lot. We drove it up here---they wouldn't let us ride in the ambulance wit' you.' Killa explained.

"We?"

"Yeah---me, LaLa, Ciara the rest of 'em. They went home though." Killa shrugged and furled her brow.

"Okay, that's cool. But when ya'll leave, leave my keys."

"Hold up, Ball---then how we gonna get home?"

"Yeah, how we gonna get home, Ball?" Ciara exclaimed, looking at him with pleading eyes.

"How am I goin' to get home?" Ball fumed. His EKG monitor beeping feverishly.

"Come on, Ball---you ain't getting' out for a couple of days. You've got a hose in your dick. The doctor said one of the billets went into your stomach, ricocheted off your tailbone and hit your bladder," LaLa was attempting to be sympathetic as she explained his condition. "The other bullet tore through your thigh muscle. You're gonna have to get your legs back under you so you can walk---so you know you can't drive right now."

"Ain't nothin' going to happen to yo' car," Killa insisted.

"I know---'cause my ride ain't leaving the parking lot until they release me from here!"

"Don't be like that, Ball." Ciara's tone was solemn.

"Be like what? Ya'll ain't getting ready to be drivin' my shit all over Monroe wit' all types of niggaz in my shit---so that's dead!"

LaLa smacked her lips in protest. "Ain't nobody gonna have no all types of niggaz in yo' ride, stop trippin'," she replied.

"This nigga is a straight clown," Killa retorted as she strutted away from the bed. "Now he tough---shoulda been tough when you *was* in *dhat* motel room *pissin'* on *yo' self.* Scared to death."

"Fuck you, bitch! They had pistols!" Ball shouted, raising up in the bed. "If I'da had a pistol---

"You *wouldna* did a *muthaphukkin' thang.* Pussy!" Killa's words struck his spine like shards of ice as she interrupted. Ball fell back on the bed and stared at the ceiling---saying nothing. "Take your fuckin' keys!"

Killa flung the car-keys at him. They clanged loudly as they bounced off his chest.

*********************************************************

Look, man---ya'll, shit *finna* go down. Ain't no bitchin' up or backing out," Axe said forcefully.

"Corey!" Sleepy blurted with laughter.

"What fuck you *hollerin'* Corey for?" Corey exclaimed as he passed the blunt to Man.

"'Cause we know yo' ass will bitch up." Sleepy said matter-of-factly. "Remember when we was gon' run up in Betty Anne's trap---you was like, nah, that's my fourth cousin or some shit--- her and Nicky good people. That nigga Nicky built like the Mucinex man an' he smells like burnt aluminum!"

The thugs laughed loudly.

"Nah, real talk. My grandma said they like my fourth cousin or some shit. Fourth or fifth---she's my grandma's father-in-law's daughter or some shit." Corey argued.

"Hold up---what you do?! Tell your grandma we was gonna rob her?!'

"Yep." Sleepy interjected with more laughter.

"Uh, *nawh*! I didn't do no shit like that."

"Yeah, you did." Axe said. His tone as cold as his stare---his index finger pointing in Corey's face.

"What the fuck ever! What we *waitin'* on?" Corey was desperate to change the subject.

"We waiting on you to go to the wizard and get some courage--- you scary-ass nigga." Sleepy said curtly. More laughter erupted. This time from Sleepy, Axe and Man.

"Fuck you. Nigga." Corey pouted.

Man stomped out the blunt remnant under his shoe and nodded to Axe. "A'ight, let's get it," Axe commanded coolly.

"What about masks? We ain't got no masks," Corey announced as they moved down the dimly lit walkway that led to Erica's apartment.

"You stupid," Sleepy remarked. "They ain't gonna open the door if they see a muthaphukka in a mask. Besides---what they gon' do? Go to the po-lice and say they got jacked for dope and money made from *sellin'* dope?"

"Oh---okay." Corey's brow furled as he acted as if he understood. "Wait! Ain't they still---

"Shut up," Axe demanded as he stuffed his fists into the weighed-down front-pocket of his navy-blue hoodie. And trekked on. Within minutes the four scofflaws were standing on Erica's front porch, mumbling, and whispering about the particulars of the heist about to take place. Sleepy rang the doorbell anxiously---and they waited.

Finally, the porch light came on and Sleepy could see an object obstruct the peephole. Someone's face, no doubt.

"Who is it?" A female voice asked dryly, yet jovially.

"You know who it is---you lookin' right at me!" Sleepy barked before lowering his tone. "Dumb-ass-bitch."

"Excuse me! What was that? Came the voice from the other side of the door. It was obvious that it was Erica's voice.

"Open the door!"

"*Taaay!*" Erica yelled as she opened the door, D'Eric and Nerica nestled in her arms. Smelling of bubble bath and baby powder. Both children appeared ready for bed, undisturbed by their mother's loudness. Nerica yawned adorably. "*Taaaay!* Sleepy here to see you!"

Tasia sauntered into the living room with Omarion on her puny hip. "Let him in,' she instructed. Seeing that her friend had restricted the hooligan to the doorway.

Sleepy forced himself through the door, his clique of robbers in tow. "Un-unh," Erica persisted as she tried to block the home evasion with her body and children.

"Where the stash at?" Axe asked vehemently. Before he could remove the gun from his hoodie Corey was brandishing a weathered Bauer .25 automatic. Man had a Heckler & Koch 9mm submachine gun which he thrust into Erica's face.

"Ain't no stash," Erica cried as she stumbled backward.

"Stop playin' Axe! Don't play like that!" Tasia yelled. But Erica knew from the look in his eyes that he was not playing---he was dead serious.

"I'm tellin' ya'll straight up---ain't no stash!" Erica was now in tears, having been weary of Sleepy's earlier presence she had removed the dope and most of the cash from her apartment---now she was regretting having done so.

Seeing their mother cry, the kids, themselves began to cry hysterically.

"Ya'll *scarin'* the babies, put them guns up," Tasia scowled as she naively put her hand on the barrel of Man's gun.

***Phop! Phop! Phop! Phop!*** Erica released a deafening scream as blood splattered from Tasia and Omarion onto her and her children. The impact of the bullets knocked Tasia's now lifeless body, along with her child into the recliner.

***Phop! Phop! Phop! Phop! Phop! Phop---Phop!*** The submachine gun shots were followed by heavy breathing and thudding hearts. But it was not the heavy breathing and thudding hearts of Erica and her innocent children---their hearts no longer beat. Erica, Nerica and D'Eric lie dead on the floor---innocent children still in their mother's arms, blood pooling beneath Erica's body. Her eyes blank. Staring at the nothingness and everything that was death.

Axe, Sleepy and Corey stared at Man and the smoking gun barrel in awe. Sleepy's nose twitched from the stench of burnt gunpowder. Man's eyes were wide and wily.

"What the fuck you do?" Corey exclaimed, looking down at the corpses.

"Made dis shit easy." Man said coldly. The fact that he had spoken frightened everyone, even Axe.

"Nah, Man—what the fuck you do that for?!" Sleepy looked as if he would cry. "You ain't have to do that."

"Straight up, you didn't." Axe's tone was somber. "Just some bitches and *dhey* kids---that's all. Easy lick!"

"Ya'll *bullshittin'!* You need to be lookin' for the stash! You know these nosey muthaphukkaz heard the shots," Man insisted. "Somebody gon' call the police!"

Axe and Sleepy adhering to Man's *gun talk* rather than his actual words ran back towards the bedroom and kitchen and began ransacking the apartment.

"This ain't right! Shit wasn't *s'posed* to go down like dis," Corey ranted. "We need to be getting' the fuck up *outta* here---muthaphukkaz probably already done called the police. We just gon' stand here and wait on *'em* to come!"

Corey was sweating profusely and shaking---the small caliber weapon clutched tightly in his chubby hand. His ears were still ringing from the gunfire, but he could hear the muffled clamor of dishes and the clanging of pots and pans coming from the kitchen and the slamming and sliding of drawers coming from the bedroom. Corey refused to move from where he stood, he couldn't.

"Yo! Ain't shit here!" Sleepy yelled from the kitchen.

"She said it wasn't no stash---she said that," Corey continued. "You know she wasn't gonna lie *wit'* a *fuckin'* gun in her face!"

"You need to shut the fuck up!" Man said through clenched teeth.

It was apparent to Corey that Man was agitated---he had spoken more in the last ten minutes then he had spoken in the past year.

In the bedroom Axe was growing frantic, he had flipped over the mattresses, searched through countless shoe boxes only to find a rubber-banded stack of cash, maybe a thousand dollars. And less than a gram of marijuana residue.

*Damn, little shorty wasn't lying*, he thought as he scoured the room. One thing was certain---if he had been a dope fiend, he would have found Erica's bedroom to be a dope fiend's paradise despite there being no dope. She had enough new clothes and shoes to open her own retail store.

"Let's roll! Ain't shit in here!" Axe shouted as he found himself staring at Erica's dresser-mirror which was covered with pictures---pictures of her posed provocatively, pictures of her and Tasia together, taken in the photo booth at Chuck-E-Cheese, taken at the club. Pictures of her and Nathan, him in his drab prison browns ad crispy New Balance sneakers. A handmade, prison-crafted Mother's Day card taped to the mirror. There was still an uncovered space on the mirror, large enough for one to see his own reflection---what Axe saw was demonic.

"Let's roll!" Axe shouted, snapping out of his momentary trance.

"We waitin' on you!" Sleepy hollered from the living room.

The jack boys fled from the apartment in a clumsy heap, knocking over trashcans and causing a disturbance. Dogs barked, apartment lights came on and eyes peered through window-blinds.

*********************************************************
**

Ralph sat in his apartment stripped of his jewelry and his pride---he watched the morning news intently as the reporter broke the story live from the crime scene. He knew the area---Grace Gardens.

"Yes, Anna---this is a tragic story, two young mothers, along with their infant children were brutally murdered in their apartment on Monroe's Southside in what police believe was a robbery attempt. But there has been speculation that the murders may have been drug related. Police have identified the two young mothers as twenty-year-old Erica Claiborne and nineteen-year-old Tasia Gaskin. We do not know the exact ages or names of the three children murdered, but we can tell you they were of infant and toddler age. We will keep you updated as police provide us with more information," the frail white female reporter spoke meticulously even though she appeared frozen as she stood in front of the taped-off apartment on Maurice Street. "We do know that one of the women---Tasia Gaskin, has an arrest from two years ago for that shoplifting and misdemeanor possession of marijuana. Witnesses say that they saw what appeared to be four black men in dark clothing running away from the apartment shortly after shots were fired. I've also been told by residents that the apartment where the victims were murdered is a known *drug house* and police will not confirm whether it is or isn't. I was told that this case is priority."

"Thank you, Susan…

Ralph became oblivious of the news broadcast on his widescreen Smart TV. "It was Axe an' them niggaz!!" He exclaimed, forcing the clipped ears of the Pitbull resting on the floor to prick in his direction. "I know it was them grimy ass niggaz! They violated code! Real stick up niggaz don't murder women or kids!"

"Anyone with any information related to this crime are urged to contact Crime Stoppers," Anna, the in-studio reporter added.

Ralph quickly scooped up his cellphone and began dialing the number given---he wiped the corners of his mouth as the phone rang. "Hey---yeah, I know who killed them two girls an' them kids on Maurice Street. I know where one of them live, too. Names? Nah---I don't know they real names---I know they street names."

**********************************************************

It did not take detectives long to apprehend three of their suspects---Axe, they had picked up at home in the bed with Tashay. Detective Greene had enlisted S.W.A.T. for Axe's apprehension, purposely making sure that the 4a.m. arrest was a brutal one that utilized everything the team had to offer---battering ram, flash-bang canisters, tear gas canisters and a beanbag round from 12-gauge shotgun.

Sleepy had been apprehended leaving the home of one his estranged girlfriends shortly after 7a.m. After begging his way into her home, Sleepy had sexed her, snorted coke until his nose bled, then confessed his transgressions. While he was showering, she had called the police---nothing worse than a lover scorn.

Corey Smith was the only one whose full government name the informant had provided and he had been arrested at his grandmother's home where he lived---he had been picked up just fifteen minutes after Axe had been taken into custody. Det. Greene and his colleagues had been unable to question Corey---he had been crying hysterically since they had placed handcuffs on him. So, they were going to wait until a respectable hour and bring his grandmother down to the station. Allow her to lull a confession out of him. He was weak, and their *Ace* in the hole.

*****************************************************************
********

Axe sat in the tiny beige room rubbing his chest which still ached from the beanbag blast he had taken. He looked at the mirrored window. "Ay! Ya'll see this shit?! I been tryin' to get some medical attention---*dhey* won't give it to me! I need medical attention!" Axe yelled at the detective.

"What about those two girls and those three babies?! You think they needed some medical attention?" Greene asked with one hand on his hip, the other fingering his striped tie as he stood over Axe. His overweight frame and the gold shield encased in leather on his waist his only weapon of intimidation.

"Man---I don't know what the hell *talkin'* about," Axe said angrily. Looking at the detective for a split-second, then looking down at the floor. "I don't know what you talkin' about, no two girls or no kids!"

"I think you do, Alexander."  The detective's tone was smug.

"My name Axe! Axe the Great! And I ain't kill nobody! I wasn't even on Maurice Street an' you ain't find no machine gun in my crib!"

Bravado is sometimes a weakness, the detective thought as he smiled at Axe. Both hands now in the pockets of his charcoal grey slacks. He then let himself out of the room and locked Axe in with his thoughts.

"Did you hear that?" Det. Greene exclaimed as he slapped hi-fives to the two other detectives working the case with him---Yates and Smitts. "If he wasn't there than where the hell was he?"

The detectives laughed heartily.

"Well, we know he was there, and we know what type of weapon it was. He confirmed all that---he even confirmed that he wasn't the shooter," Yates stated before biting into a custard-filled éclair.

"You don't think he's the shooter?" Greene frowned.

"Did he tell you he was the shooter?" Yates asked rhetorically, licking his fingers greedily.

"He's got a point," Det. Smitts added---as he eyed the last éclair in the box.

"Well, I'm not *buyin'* that the cry baby is the shooter."

"Corey?!" Smitts interjected.

"So, you think it was Sleepy? Our man Barrow Reid?" Det. Yates scarfed down what had remained of the éclair as he waited for an answer.

"Sleepy? Nah, our man Sleepy's soft," Greene explained. "He's a pretty boy---it wasn't a forced entry, so Sleepy's how they got in."

"So, you believe Sleepy sweet talked one of the girls into letting them in?" Smitts asked. Questioning his colleague's logic.

"I know so!" Greene said as he sat down in the springy office chair, stretched his legs and clasped his hands behind his head.

"What about what the neighbors said? About there being a high level of drug traffic moving in and out of the apartment. We found a scale, baggies, cigars, and razor blades---not to mention that shoe box full of weed remnants. We know these girls weren't *bakin'* and *sellin'* cookies. You don't think that these girls were expecting these guys to come by and make a legitimate buy?" Yates scratched his balding head.

Detective Greene picked up a mugshot of Axe off a nearby desk and held it before the detectives. "Alexander Wilson---aka Axe the Great, is a known and convicted armed robber! A stick-up kid! What are they calling 'em now? A, uh---jackboy! And they went to that apartment with the intention of *jackin'* these two girls of drugs and money!"

"What about the fourth man?" Smitts asked, slumped over in his chair playing with his handcuffs.

"The fourth guy's our shooter." Greene answered.

"You really think so?" Yates smirked. He was always fascinated at how his colleague deciphered criminology.

"Yeah, and I think that way only because we know nothing about him. What we need are the lab results from the clothing we seized from Axe's place. I'm sure that the blood on the clothing is from our victims. We need to see what latent has---get some I.D. matches on the prints they lifted from the victim's place."

"You ready to talk to Sleepy?" Yates asked. Det. Greene ran his fingers across his graying crew cut and sighed.

"Naah---I think I'll let you talk to him."

Detective Yates smiled slyly and grabbed the box containing the solitary éclair as he stood and made his way to an adjacent interrogation room where Sleepy pace the thin carpet.

"Hey, Sleep'---you hungry, buddy? I brought you an éclair." Yates said pleasantly. "Have a seat."

Sleepy stared at the odd-looking detective suspiciously as he took a seat in a blue plastic chair on the other side of a tiny aluminum table. Det. Yates sat diagonal from him in a hard plastic yellow chair and slid the pastry box towards the suspect.

Sleepy eyed the chocolate frosting-covered éclair---his stomach growled loudly with hunger. "You want me to touch that box, so you can get my fingerprints off it! I ain't stupid!" He exclaimed as he shook his head.

"Now that's stupid---we already got your prints from the apartment of those two dead girls. Eat the éclair. It's not a trick."

The detective's words resonated in the pit of Sleepy's stomach, and he craved the chocolate pastry, or any food for that matter. "Sir, my fingerprints ain't in nobody's apartment. You can't believe *sh---*, you can't believe *nothin'* Reneek say, sir. She gets like that. She still mad at me for *sleepin' wit'* her sister," he pleaded.

"Do you want my help or not?" Yates asked as he scratched the back of his hairy hand.

"I want---I want your help, but I ain't done nothin', sir." Sleepy was having trouble getting his words out. Det. Yates could sense that he was nervous.

"Listen to me---we know you were in the apartment; we've got your prints. Plus, your buddy Corey already ratted you out," Yates stated calmly. Hoping that the results he awaited implicated Sleepy in some way. Abruptly, a knock came at the door.

The door creaked open and Det. Greene there straight-faced, holding a manilla folder. "Yates---I need to see you for a sec'," he said. Summoning his colleague with the folder.

"Sit tight, buddy. I'll be right back." Yates said as he closed the door behind him.

Det. Greene stood bearing a shit-eating grin.

"What's up?"

"We've got both Sleepy and Axe's prints at the crime scene. The blood on Axe's clothes was from one of our victims---the little girl," Greene announced as he slapped the folder against Det. Yates' chest. "Oh, the shell casings were clean."

"Awesome." Yates flipped through the folder like a kid with a new comic book. "I'll go in here and see if he wants to save himself."

Det. Yates entered the interrogation room and slapped the folder down on the desk. "Eat the damn éclair, Sleepy!" He yelled.

"I'm good," Sleepy replied somberly.

"Eat the damn éclair! You don't want my help! You don't want to help yourself---it may be the last éclair you eat for the next fifty years! If they don't give you the death penalty!"

"Death penalty?! What you talkin' 'bout?" Sleepy felt feverish---faint.

"We've got your prints all in the apartment! We've got Axe's prints! Blood from one of the victims on his clothes! Which means he was probably the shooter---but he and Corey are saying you're the shooter! So, what's gonna happen when we pick up the fourth man?! I'll tell you what! He's gonna say Sleepy's the shooter! He's gonna say Barron Reid is the shooter!! He's gonna say you shot two young mothers and three innocent kids! Defenseless women and kids!' Yates yelled and snatched his tie loose melodramatically.

Sleepy's shoulders slumped, then his head dropped---the burden of guilt weighing heavy on the young hooligan and Det. Yates knew it.

"Who's the fourth guy, Sleep'? Who was the shooter?! Help me help you!"

Sleepy sighed and shook his head.

"Come on, Sleep'---I'm trying to help you, buddy. Help me help you," Yates pleaded. Placing his hand on Sleepy's shoulder. He could feel his suspect's fear---he was trembling.

Sleepy looked up at him. Those eyes that had seduced so many females, those bedroom eyes that had seen the insides of so many bedrooms, were filled with tears and defeat. His mouth was open, but no words escaped.

"Come on, Sleep'---buddy."

Sleepy cleared his throat and wiped his eyes. "I was in the apartment---I was in the apartment earlier yesterday because I spent the night *wit'* Tay on Friday, rather Saturday morning. We left the club together. Me, her, Erica, and the dude Erica was *fu--- messin' wit'*, sir. I ain't do nothing, sir," he insisted. "That's why my fingerprints was in there. People seen me leave Saturday, it was 'bout two o'clock. I stopped an' talked to Deanna for three minutes, her grandma sittin' on the porch being nosey. She saw me."

**************************************************************************

*"Lawwwwd! Lawwwd*! It ain't *ri-i-ihgt!* Them babies didn't do nothin' to nobody! All them my babies---Tay! Omarion! Nerica! D'Eric! Erica! All them was my ba-bies! And they didn't deserve this! They didn't *de-servvvve* to die like that! Who would kill lil' babies?!?" Pam screamed—standing in front of Eric's crime scene tape-covered apartment with a group of mournful family and friends.

A group of young ruffians stood at the end of cul-de-sac smoking a blunt and watching the spectacle. At the sight of them Pam became more enraged and stormed towards them. "You sorry bastards! You probably know who did it! You need to say somethin'! They killed three lil' babies! My daughter! An' her best friend! Ya'll know who did it! Ya'll probably did it!" Pam screamed as she pointed her finger and hiked up her low-rise jeans. Her face contorted with hurt and loss. No longer appearing as the older, yet young looking attractive woman that they lusted over.

One of the ruffians, a yellow-faced, teardrop-tattooed youth sucked his teeth and gave Pam a malicious glance. *"Yoooou!* You killed my babies! Coward! Coward-ass muthaphukka!" She screamed in his face.

"He ain't kill nobody, Ms. Pam. None of us did," a dark-skinned youth in a black hoodie and navy-blue Dickies coveralls explained in a sympathetic tone as he stepped between the two. "Erica, Tay an' dem was good people."

"They was wasn't they?" She muttered as she put her arms around his neck and began to sob. All of the ruffians shed their stoic demeanors as they watched Pam grieve.

■■■■■■■■■■■■■■■■■■■■■■■■■■■■■■■■■■■■■■■■■■■■■■■■■■■■

Tashay honked the horn and hit the brake pedal, bringing the BMW to an abrupt halt. Man's uncle, who was known as Uncle Junior brought the beat-up work truck to a halt as well. Tashay lowered her window, allowing the frigid air to invade the inner warmth of her vehicle. "Uncle Junior!" She shouted so that she could be heard over the disturbance that escaped the truck's muffler. "You *seen* Man?"

"Man?! *Naw*, I ain't *seent* him!" The burly, bugged-eyed man replied.

"If you see him---tell him the police picked up Axe early this mornin'!" Tashay now had her whole head out the window. "They set off tear gas in da house---shot Axe wit' one of those beanbag things! They took a bag of his clothes, too!"

"Hush up! You serious?!" Uncle Junior exclaimed.

"Yes! They had da S.W.A.T. team all in my house!"

"Well, I'm headed over to his mama's---she might know where he is, if he ain't over dhere! I'll tell 'em what's goin' on!"

"I already been by his mama's house! She gone to church! Man wasn't there, I talked to his sister, Kamesha!"

"Oh, okay! What's all dis about anyway?" Uncle Junior asked, but he already knew. Man had told him and begged for his help. That's why now Man lie n the bed of his uncle's truck wrapped in quilts and concealed by wheelbarrows---headed for Pageland, South Carolina.

"The detectives really didn't say much! I asked but they wouldn't tell me nothin'---da *muthaphukkas* was actin' real sour!"

"If I see Man I'll let him know, you hear?!"

With that said Uncle Junior backed his truck out of the driveway hastily---so recklessly that Tashay had to quickly throw her BMW in reverse to avoid a collision.

Tashay's cellphone chirped and vibrated on the passenger seat. She quickly picked it up and put it on *speaker*---then placed it back on the seat. "Hello—what's up, Theresa?"

"I'on't know. You tell me?"

"I don't know what to tell you, the police picked up Axe early this morning---they wouldn't tell me why. I called the jail, twice, he's not there---that's what they tell me. "Tashay said dryly.

"*Gurl*, is you for real? You 'on't know why Axe in jail?!"

"They wouldn't tell me nothin'!" Tashay was growing angry with Theresa's idiotic questions.

"Um---Axe, Sleepy an' Corey killed Erica, Tasia and they babies! They picked Sleepy up leaving Reneek house---I heard she called the police. They got Corey at his grandma's," Theresa said matter-of-factly.

"No fuck he didn't! Axe wouldn't do no shit like that! And Sleepy and Corey damn sure *wouldn't*! Shut the hell up *wit'* that shit! I ain't goin' for that!" Tashay yelled at the cellphone as she drove.

"Erica an' Tay dead! Them three babies dead! Erica's two kids and Tasia's one---they dead! That's what the police picked Axe an' them up for!"

Tashay slammed on the brake, just avoiding running a redlight and into traffic.

"I ain't heard nothin' about nobody getting killed, and Axe do a lot of shit, but he wouldn't kill no females or they kids---you lyin'."

"Why *I'ma* lie *'bout* some shit like that! It's been on the news! You ain't heard nothin' about it, *'cause* you think you better than *er'body* else--- *'cause* you think you better than er'body else--- *'cause* you went to school an' you don't live in the projects! You just live two streets aways." Theresa was blunt.

"Shut up! Shut up! Shut up!"

***************************************************************

"Mrs. Smith, I apologize for taking you away from your home for this, but we're trying to help your grandson, Corey." Det. Greene said safely. "He won't talked to us, ma'am---he's been crying since we brought him in."

"*I'ma* give him somethin' to cry about---*pullin'* me away from Jesus. I ain't missed a full Sunday service in over twenty-five years! I'm on the usher broad. I been an usherette for the las' twenty years come this July."

Det. Greene smiled politely at the squat, brown, spunky elderly woman and led her to her to the interrogation room where her grandson was being held.

"Mr. Greene?"

"Yes, ma'am."

"Do you attend church on Sundays?"

"Honestly, ma'am---it's been a while since I've seen the inside of a church on a Sunday, or any day for that matter. The life of a homicide detective is very busy."

"Too busy for God?"

"No ma'am. I listen to the pastors on the AM radio stations from time to time." Greene was impressed by her candidness.

"You said *you's* a how-many-sides detective?"

"Homicide---murder. I investigate murders, ma'am. And right now, I'm investigating the murders of two young mothers and three young children---babies."

'Je-sus! *Lawwd* no!" Mrs. Smith cried out. "My Corey ain't done no such thang! That's the work of the devil! Where my Corey!?!"

"Right inn here, ma'am." Greene said, opening the door and escorting her in.

"Corey! Corey!"

"Grandma!" Corey cried, his eyes red and swollen. His face plastered with tears and sweat. Without warning Mrs. smith began pummeling him with her purse.

"You! Better! These! Police! What! They! Wanna! Know!" Mrs. Smith shouted as she beat her grandson.


Det. Greene allowed Mrs. Smith to release her frustration and motherly intimidation for a few minutes before he stopped her.

"Corey---I brought your sweet grandmother down here, because I know she loves you and you love her---and she raised you to do the right thing. And I know you want to do the right thing, don't you?" Greene was coaxing his suspect as best he knew how.

"Ye-ye-yeah!" Corey blurted, trying to control his hyperventilating. His grandmother hit him again with her purse.

"What you say?" She snapped.

"Yes sir."

"Corey, I *'clare fo'* lord---if you don't tell Mr. Greene what happened you gon' meet your maker this day, hear, you hear me?"

"Ye-yes ma'am," he muttered.

"Okay, Corey, *buddy*---have a seat, then tell me what happened when you gon' meet your maker this day, hear, you hear me?"

"Ye-yes ma'am," he muttered.

"Okay, Corey, buddy---have a seat, then tell me what happened you gon' meet your maker this day, hear, you hear me?"

"Ye-yes ma'am," he muttered.

"Okay, Corey, *buddy*---have a seat, then tell me what happened when you got to Erica's and who was with you?" Det. Greene said as he offered Mrs. Smith a seat, then sat down himself.

Corey exhaled deeply. "It was me, Axe, Sleepy and Man---

"Who's man? What's his real name?" Greene interrupted.

"Man?! Ain't that Beverly Gordon's grandboy? Angie's boy?"

"Yes ma'am," Corey shook violently. "Man's name is Greg Alston, he's one of my *partnas*---friends. Uh, Sleepy knocked on the door. Erica let us in, we all went in."

"Why'd you all go there?" Greene asked, fighting in the urge to smile.

"Sleepy mess *wit'* Tay, you mean Tasia?" Greene interrupted as he took notes.

"Yes sir---Tasia. So, he was like let's go see what's up *wit'* Tay--- Tasia an' Erica."

"So, you guys didn't go there to rob them?" Greene gave Corey a puzzled look.

"No sir."

"Go ahead."

"So, we get inside, Erica standing there *wit'* her kids in her arms---she call Tay, Tay come into the living room holdin' her kid. Then Sleepy, Axe and Man start *whisperings'*---I couldn't hear what they *was* saying, but suddenly Man an' Axe pull out guns, but Man start *shootin'*---it happened so quick."

"Who did he start shooting at?"

"Erica, Tay---all of 'em."

"All of them?"

"The kids, Erica, Tay an' the kids," Corey's tone was somber as tears streamed down his face.

"Did you and Sleepy have guns?" Det. Greene asked with a stern look.

"No sir."

"If you didn't go there to rob them than why was the apartment torn up and you *alls* fingerprints all over the place?"

"No sir! Not my fingerprints, I didn't touch nothin'!" Corey cried excitedly "I ran out---if they robbed the spot, I didn't know nothin' about it!"

"Corey, you need to be honest with me. And you need to be honest with your grandmother and yourself."

"I-I-I'm *bein'* honest with you, sir."

'No, you're not." Det. Greene said bluntly.

"Corey!" Mrs. Smith cocked her head and gave the grandson she had raised since he was nine years old a sideways glare.

"They went through the house an' started lookin' for money and weed. Erica be tryin' to hustle a lil' weed, but wasn't nothin' in there.'

"Who went through the apartments looking for money and weed?" Greene asked as he sat back in his seat and folded his arms across his chest.

'Sleepy an' Axe---I think Seepy went in the kitchen and Axe went to check the bedrooms. I ain't sure because I ran out."

"Corey---do you want to spend the rest of your life in prison?"

"No, no, sir." Corey shook his head continuously.

"Tell the truth, son. We've got witnesses that saw four men running away from the crime scene, not three, but four."

"I, I mean---I ran out before everybody. We was runnin' together, all us, but, uh, I was in the front," Corey insisted.

He was sweating profusely now and shaking uncontrollably.

"So, what did Sleepy, and Axe take out of the apartment?"

"Nobody got any weed or money.

"Not that I know, but---Erica wasn't holdin' nothing. She said, ain't no stash."

"When do dead girls talk? If Sleepy and Axe searched the apartment after---," Det. Greene looked down at his note pad. "Man, Greg Alston shot the victims than when did she tell you all that there ain't no stash?"

Detective Yates who had heard everything said during Corey's interrogation had already put out an APB for Greg Alston, now he was going in to interrogate Axe.

"Get up," Yates said. Tapping the sole of Axe's sneaker with his loafer. Axe was asleep on the floor. "I need to talk to you."

"Look, man---I ain't got shit to talk about. I ain't kill nobody, so you either gon' let me go or lock me up," Axe sounded disgruntled.

"Oh, you'll be going to jail, but how long is the question---six hundred months? Or a thousand months?" Axe got up off the floor and looked at the detective with wide-eyed bewilderment.

"Yeah, the fourth guy—Greg Alston, you all call him Man---your friends Corey and Sleepy already gave him up as the shooter and you as the mastermind! We've got your prints all in Erica' bedroom! We know that you went there with intentions to rob those girls for drugs and money, but there wasn't any. Erica told you guys there *ain't no stash*, but Man shot them anyway---in cold. You used Sleepy to get you all in the apartment."

"I ain't use nobody! I ain't mastermind a muthaphukkin' thing---point blank!" Axe screamed into the face of the detective. He was angry. He knew someone had talked---there was a snitch in his crew, and he knew that most likely it was Corey.

"Alexander Wilson. You're such a tough guy," Yates said dryly with a simper. "Five counts of first-degree murder, five counts of armed robbery---whether it's home invasion or burglary---you've done time before---does Alexander Wilson with all the time you're going to get---does Alexander remain Axe the Great, or become Alexis the Black Bitch?"

"Fuck you pussy! I ain't nobody's bitch!" Axe charged the detective---his rage being recorded by the camera on the other side of the mirrored glass. Two detectives rushed into the interrogation room and pulled Axe off of Det. Yates.

*******************************************************************

"I got one more question for you. The gun, what k---

"Heckler and Koch, nine---machine gun type," Corey blurted before Det. Greene could finish the question.

Det. Greene looked at Corey's grandmother, took her hands in his own. "Ma'am, he's going to be charged---and he'll eventually go away to prison. I'll ask the DA to take into consideration that he cooperated with my investigation. "I promise," he said reassuringly.

"Thank you, Mr. Greene. Now I'ma ask a favor of you," Mrs. Smith said, looking at him with warm jaundice-colored eyes.

"Anything, ma'am."

"Lord knows I ain't gon' live long enough to see him come out. I'm all the real family he got----look in on him, you hear?"

"Yes ma'am."


******************* 18 MONTHS LATER*******************


"Alexander Wilson---you've agreed to testify for the state, thereby avoiding the death penalty. And you've requested a prayer for judgement. Son---" The judge removed his glasses and eyed Axe apathetically. 'You and your little buddies took the lives of three innocent children and their young mothers. Heinous. I don't care what they sold or how much of it they sold---or how much ill-gotten money they had or didn't have. Now you want prayer---I'm a judge, not a preacher. I go to church very seldom, but I do fear God. The Bible says do not despise a thief if he steals to satisfy his hunger, but if the thief is caught, he must repay it seven folds. I hereby sentence you to a combined sentence of seven hundred and seventy-one months. It's going to be hell in there---fear God."

"Snitch!" Someone shouted. Mutters and *oohs* filled the courtroom.

The judge's sentence along with the announcement made by the street crier resonated in Axe's head before he fainted. Ralph who stood in the back of the courtroom smiled triumphantly as the courtroom roared with mixed emotions.

The bailiffs revived Axe and escorted him out of the courtroom and placed him in a holding cell. There he paced the floor thinking more about Corey's sentence than his own---the day before the exact same judge had pleasantly accepted Corey's plea agreement for two hundred and forty months, Det. Greene had shaken his hand and patted him on the back before he was escorted out of the courtroom.

He thought about Sleepy, but only for a second---Sleepy was back at the Union County Jail playing Spades and listening to the rumors that his long-time friends, now co-defendants had agreed to testify against him once he went on trial. Rumors he was beginning to believe were true, even though he did not want to believe them. Especially the rumors that Axe had *turned state*.

Man---Greg Alston had gained national attention. His profile had come across television screens of millions that watched AMW. He was still on the run.

# HOW MIAMI MOVE

"So, what Monroe like?" Yami asked as he spotted Hot Shot who was completing his third rep with three hundred and five pounds. His southern drawl was thick and syrupy---that of a true Miami native.

"It's a'ight. It damn sure ain't like down your way---I'm tryna come down there an' get some sunshine, *ses* and sex," Hot Shot answered as he put the weighted bar back on the rack and sat up. Yami laughed.

"You want you a lil'*shone*, lil' *chonga*---lil' *city girl* for *sho'*, huh?" Yami continued to laugh.

"Hell yeah!" Hot Shot was now laughing as other inmates moved about the weight pile.

Yami, which was not his given name and was abbreviation for *Miami*, was a very jovial individual when he was not provoked. His tar-black revealed some Haitian heritage and a love for Miami, Florida's sunbaked streets. He was tall and lanky, standing six-foot-two with wick-locks that resembled tree roots and a bush-gold grill---*bush-gold* having an orangish-gold color that was distinct trademark of Miami natives. Still his entire mouth gleamed brightly.

Despite having the appearance of a jovial black palm tree, Yami was a twenty-six-year-old product of his environment---a desolated and violent soul hailing from Miami, Dade County's infamous Pork'n' Bean Projects. He was now just days away from completing a twenty-nine-month sentence for shooting into an occupied dwelling. A charge he had obtained at strip club in Charlotte.

Hot Shot was damn near right at home at Brown Creek Correctional Facility in Anson County---he was from Monroe, North Carolina which was just thirty-five minutes away. Having been at the prison a year before Yami had arrived, Hot Shot was well established, and the two ruffians had clicked immediately.

Hot Shot got off the weight bench and flexed his muscles as he tightened the belt on his brown prison-issued pants. He then grabbed his t-shirt off the bench and used it to wipe the sweat from his face and shoulders. The forty-four months he had spent working out was making his forty-four-to-fifty-eight-month sentence worth it---not only was he a better criminal, but he now had the muscle tone of a professional bodybuilder, at least in his upper body.

Hot Shot, now twenty-four had been taken from the streets when he was twenty years old and had been fiending for the streets ever since. Fiending to bring havoc to his Southside neighborhood---Maurice Street Projects. Now the notorious Grace Gardens.

"I'm thirsty, you want a soda?" Yami asked he patted his pockets for his canteen card.

"*Dhat's* what up. Get me a Sprite." Hot Shot said as he stuffed his massive head and arms through the openings in the once white t-shirt.

"I was gon' give you my card an' let you get 'em," Yami said with a sly grin. "An' get me a bag of chips. *Dhat* should kill it."

"Ain't no way!" Hot Shot exclaimed with a grin as he looked at the lengthy line of inmates awaiting canteen. "*Dhat* line longer than a muthaphukka."

"Dhat shit crazy, Hot Shot! Why *you can't* go?"

"Man, I'm tryna hurry up and hit this shower---go 'head. The line ain't dhat long."

"Dhat shit crazy---next run on you."

"No doubt." Hot Shot smirked, line, pulling up his pants every few seconds. Hot Shot then headed to the dormitory, the stench of the neighboring farm familiar and no longer an issue.

∙∙∙∙∙∙∙∙∙∙∙∙∙∙∙∙∙∙∙∙∙∙∙∙∙∙∙∙∙∙∙∙∙∙∙∙∙∙∙∙∙∙∙∙∙∙∙∙∙∙∙∙∙∙∙∙∙∙∙∙∙∙∙∙∙∙∙∙∙∙∙

Hot Shot had showered, lotioned and dressed by the time Yami returned with his drunk---the twenty-ounce beverage in his back pocket forcing his pants to sag even lower than usual. His own drink and bag of chips occupying his hands. "*Dhat* line long as fuck," Yami announced as he handed Hot Shot the drink and sat down at the foot of his cohort's bed.

"Good lookin' out," Hot Shot said as he accepted the soda and placed the magazine, he was reading next to him on the bed.

"No problem---you just make *sho* you look out for me when I come through Monroe," Yami crumpled the empty potato chip bag in his hand. His remark caused Hot Shot to suck his teeth.

"Stop bullshittin'---you know you ain't comin' to the *Roe*."

"Dhat's my word, my nigga! I'ma come look you up. Shit---you get out next month. I'm goin' to Miami, but I'ma shoot back up this way after 'bout three or fou' months."

"Dhat's what's up," Hot Shot said giving his associate a pound-handshake. "But you ain't slick nigga---you comin' back down this way to see dhat broad."

"What *broad*?" Yami asked with a gleaming grin.

"What broad," Hot Shot mimicked. "*Muthaphukka*, you know what broad---Ms. Walls, nigga."

"The C.O. chick?!" Yami laughed, as did Hot Shot. "I *ain't thainkin' 'bout dhat* city girl. She got a *donk* on her though."

· · · · · · · · · · · · · · · · · · · · · · · · · · · · · · · · · · · · · · · · · · · · · ·

## <u>4 MONTHS LATER</u>

Hot Shot sat on his aunt's porch at the corner of Maurice Street and Green Street, the apartment where he had been raised most of his life. He had been home only three months and he was enjoying every minute of it.

He sat splitting and spitting sunflower seeds, amazed at how many of the young, under-developed girls had grown into overdeveloped young ladies. Their bodies exaggerated with womanly curves. Most of the females his age was still thick and voluptuous, but some had developed small poaches from the two or three children they had given birth to during his stint in prison. There were still a lot of females Hot Shot had not seen since being home and a lot of females that had not seen him.

"Ooooh! There go my baby!" Dejanee screamed as she ran towards Hot Shot. He eased off the porch smoothly and caught her in his arms. "When you get home?"

"A few months ago," Hot Shot answered, holding her tight around her slim waist and her thick mahogany legs wrapped around his waist and her arms around his thick neck. She smacked her luscious lips loudly. "You ain't gon' grab my ass?" She asked with excited frustration. He quickly moved his hands to her humongous derriere as she held his neck tightly.

"You done got big Hot Shot," she purred into his ear.

"You done got big, too."

They both laughed as he squeezed her plump ass before placing her firmly on the ground. Dejanee stood before him in a pink short-cropped tunic, *coochie-cutting* denim short-shorts and a pair of Vince Camuto-Bendsen wedge-sandals. Her naturally long, black hair was ghettoized with pink track snippets added for flair.

Dejanee's wedge-sandals almost had her succulent five-five frame elevated to Hot Shot's height of five-foot-eleven. Hot Shot could not take his eyes of her thighs---he almost did not notice the brilliantly painted *donk* blasting vintage Trick Daddy that came to a halt in front of his aunt's apartment. A group of females stopped to admire the high-riding Chevy as they slurped on Creamsicles to cool their hot bodies---the sun was blazing.

Before the wick-lock-haired ruffian could climb down from the '87 Chevy, Hot Shot spotted the gleaming bush-gold grill. Yami ---true to his Dade County roots was fashioned in a lime green Amiri graphic tee, white Dickie shorts, no socks, and a pair of lime green Dior sneakers. He swaggered across the small lawn, blacker than ever. "What's *happppenin'* my nig'?" Yami exclaimed as he greeted Hot Shot with *dap* and a hug.

"What's good, nigga?"

"I told you I was *comin'* for *sho',*" Yami said with a smile. Dejanee immediately noticed his out-of-town swagger and deep southern drawl, unlike the normal North Carolina- South Carolina drawls she was used to. She was interested.

"Hot Shot, who's your friend?" She interrupted as she poked out her hip alluringly.

"Oh, this my man, Yami---we met in prison. He's a real nigga." Yami beamed with pride at the urban accolade bestowed upon him---it was the highest honor on the streets. Dejanee wanted more. "Where h from?" She asked.

"I'm from Dade County----Miami," he announced with pride as he rocked on his heels and eyed Dejanee lustfully. Then her purposely directed his attention back to Hot Shot---he reached into his pocket and brought out a small stack of fifty- and twenty-dollar bills. "Dhat's what's up--- *'preciate dhat,*" he said as he shoved the money into his own pocket.

"Hot Shot, I'ma let you talk to your friend, but I'll be back by. I'ma go call Alexis and let her know your home," Dejanee said before sauntering away.

"A'ight." Hot Shot and Yami remarked as he watched as Dejanee sashayed hard---her hips rocking from left to right as her ass bounced up and down.

"Damn, *dhat* city-girl *swol'*," Yami remarked as he watched her vanish. "*Dhat* you?"

"Nah, dhat ain't me, but she can be. I'll knock her down."

They both laughed as a flock of kids gathered around the colorful *donk* in amusement, some touching its wet-looking paint. In the distance the ice cream truck chimed. "Ay! Ay! Ay! Ya'll come over here away from dhat car, I'm get ya'll somethin' twenty-dollar bill from his pocket and held it high. They scurried to him anxiously. All but one, who continued to fondle the Chevy. "Ay---come over here lil' man! I'ma buy you somethin' from the ice cream truck."

The little snotty-nose, blackboy with his untied #7 Jordans peered menacingly at Hot Shot through the sunlight. "*Bish!* I ain't lil'---an' I *'on't* need you to buy me *nuffin!* My big *brotha* a dope boy!" The four-year young miscreant yelled before running away. Hot Shot almost felt bad because he knew where the misguided youth was headed, but the sincerity and sympathy quickly subsid and he laughed at the kid's comment.

"I *thaink shawty* called you a bitch. He wild as hell, ain't he," Yami said laughing hysterically as the ice cream truck turned on Green Street.

"Yeah, he is," Hot Shot said, running his hand over his freshly cut one-against-the-grain. "A'ight---ya'll come on." The group of kids huddled close to him as they walked to the curb to meet the truck as it stopped.

"*A'ight*, what ya'll want? We gon' start *wit'* you lil' momma," his tone polite.

"I want a pickled pig feet *an'* a bag of cotton candy," the chubby little girl exclaimed. Her navel peeking from beneath her Dora Explorer tank top Her body bordering obesity like so many black youths in southern ghettoes whose parents bear ignorance to the signs of sugar, fat and salt. Hot Shot smiled with that same ignorance.

"You gonna eat all dhat lil' mama?"

"Yes," she answered courteously.

"Give 'em what they want," he instructed the vendor as he handed him a twenty-dollar bill.

"What about me?" Came a sultry feminine voice from over Hot Shot's broad shoulder. He turned to find Pam Gaskin standing behind him---at thirty-five she still had it. Her thick, five-two caramel frame looked scrumptious. A white and gold Chanel scarf wrapped her head, white Chanel frames covered her face, and a white body-dress tightly covered her body---she was barefoot, her pretty toes exposed.

"What's good, Ms. Pam," Hot Shot said with a warm grin, before his face became somber. "I heard what happened---I'm sorry 'bout your loss."

"I 'preciate it," she said as she embraced him with a strained smile. It was evident she was still mourning the loss of Tasia, Omarion, Erica, D'Eric and Nerica. Her pain illustrated in the ink embedded in her flesh, their names tattooed on her neck and wrists. She stared at Yami as she hugged Hot Shot firmly. "I heard you was home---all big an' looking good. Who's your friend?"

"This my man, Yami---he from Miami," he explained as he released her supple frame. Pam for a moment refusing to let go.

"Nice to meet you, *Yami*." Pam said with a seductive smile as she shook his hand.

"Same here, Ms. Pam---right?" Yami said smoothly as he held onto her hand gingerly and peered down into her slanted eyes.

"You can call me Pam," she answered before looking over at Hot Shot. "He's cute."

Yami played the game, so he understood it---it was recognized. "You cute, too," he said coolly. Her hand still in his own. He liked that she was assertive, yet subtle. A grown woman with hers.

Pam eyed his tall, slender frame with strong desire. She was infatuated with his deep dark skin. Adored his long, rugged dreadlocks. "Yami, do you have a girlfriend?" She asked.

"Naw."

"What about a woman?"

He smiled, his grill shining. "Naw---not yet."

"Yes, you do---if you act right," she said playfully as she stared into stared into his eyes. "Hot Shot, I'm havin' a cookout. Make sure you bring Yami wit' you, please. I'm over on Hudson Street, now---you can't miss it, just follow the people. It starts at four."

"I gotcha." Hot Shot assured her.

"Yami, I hope you like to dance," she said as she escaped his grasp and gaited away.

"What's up *wit'* Pam?" Yami asked nudging his friend.

"Ms. Pam want some dick," Hot Shot explained. "Remember when my man, Boobie came in for probation violation an' he was talkin' 'bout them niggaz dhat robbed *an'* murdered them too broads and they kids?"

"Yeah, dhat was some ol' fuck shit," Yami grimaced.

"Well, one of them broads *was* her daughter, *an'* one of the kids was her grand-baby---it's been a minute, but the shit still fuck wit' her from what I hear. You know how dhat go."

"I know how dhat go---she need this Dade County dick to take her mind of thangs." The two laughed.

"So, what's up *wit'* the cookout?" Yami continued as a new blue BMW 3-Series cruised by.

"Oh, we goin' to the cookout, my nigga. I hear LaLa gonna be there---I'm tryna get at her."

"Who's LaLa?"

"The badass *yellow bone* I told you about---I was shootin' at her before I went in. The muthaphukka so thick now it don't make no sense! But she only fuck wit' dope boys, paper *chasin'* like a muthaphukka," Hot Shot explained. His voice sounding distant, as if he were off searching for the money, he needed to acquire LaLa.

"Then *dhat* mean we gotta get dhat paper my nig'---I'm here now." Yami said, giving the muscular ruffian *dap.*

"Yeah, you is, So when you gonna take me down to Miami?"

"*Cain't* do dhat." Yami 's tone was dry.

"You can't do dhat? Why not?" Hot Shot inquired with disbelief.

"Dade hot right now."

"It's *s'posed* to be, it's summertime. Plus, it's Miami."

"Naw, it's *hot*. They tryin' to say I killed somebody."

"Who is *they*?!"

"The po-lice," Yami said slow and matter-of-factly.

"Did you?" Hot Shot asked, giving Yami an awkward gaze.

"Let's go for a ride, blow *somehin'*, get something to eat befo' the cookout. Run up on some *city girls*,' Yami said changing the subject.

"Nigga, we goin' to a cookout---it's gonna be broads an' shit to eat there.

"My nig'---you hear you?" Yami asked laughing. "Plus, I'm still *makin'* up for dhat bullshit I ate for twenty-nine months. I always got room for food. *Sheeit!* And I wanna see more of Monroe. I already see it's niggas 'round here getting' money."

"Dhat's what I'm talkin' 'bout! I like how you think, my nigga!" Hot Shot was enthused. He looked at the kids---smiling faces covered with ice-cream and cotton candy. "Er'body straight?"

They all nodded their heads continuing to enjoy their treats.

"Okay---where my change?"

"I got it!!" The chubby youth exclaimed as she bit into her cotton candy-covered pickled pig foot.

"Dhat's good like dhat?" Hot Shot asked teasingly. She nodded her "yes." He and Yami both smiled. "You go 'head and keep dhat change, lil' mama."

She smiled and pranced around as Hot Shot and Yami walked towards the *donk*. "Let's shoot to Icemorelee for a lil' bit. I'll tell you how to get there," Hot Shot said.

They climbed into the lemon yellow and cherry red checkered Chevy and proceeded to the Icemorelee Neighborhood. Yami handed

Hot Shot jar of Kush and a pack of Backwoods cigars as he drove, his long black arm hanging out of the driver's side window.

∙∙∙∙∙∙∙∙∙∙∙∙∙∙∙∙∙∙∙∙∙∙∙∙∙∙∙∙∙∙∙∙∙∙∙∙∙∙∙∙∙∙∙∙∙∙∙∙∙∙∙∙∙∙∙∙∙∙∙∙∙∙∙∙∙∙∙∙∙∙

Pam had changed her outfit four times before committing to a pair of five-inch-tall coral-colored Louboutin sling-back glitter peep toes, light-colored denim short-shorts that left her ass cheeks visible and a coral camisole. Her crystal-coated YSL sunglasses resting atop her new hairdo---a caramelized pixie-cut. Her look was fierce and accentuated by minimal jewelry. A diamond tennis bracelet and initial ring her late daughter had given her.

Pam walked from the bedroom to the kitchen where her best friend Gracie was preparing the hamburger meat for the grill. "Gracie, why you chop the bell peppers so big?" She asked as she investigated the large bowl her friend was forming her patties from.

"Them peppers ain't chopped too big," Gracie insisted. "Gon' an' sit down somewhere!"

"Knock! Knock! Liquors here!" Annette yelled from the living room as she slammed the door closed.

"We in the kitchen!" Pam shouted back daintily as she grabbed a beer from the refrigerator. Then she sat down at the kitchen table and watched through the sliding glass door as three of the neighborhood *corner boys* arranged the picnic tables in the backyard.

"You lazy bitches need to be in the living room *carryin'* this box into the kitchen," Annette said as she came around the corner carrying the large box of spirits. Pam and Gracie laughed at the tiny light-skinned female as she struggled to place the box on the table. "I wish I *woulda* dropped it."

"Whatever---yo' alcoholic-ass ain't droppin' no liquour," Gracie said as she laid another hand-molded patty into a plastic see-thru container.

"Fuck you," Annette blurted. All three women laughed. Gradually the doorbell began chiming repetitiously as guests began arriving in droves, some bearing platters of food while most were empty0handed, bringing only smiles and hugs for the hostess and the rest of the guests.

Pam quickly gathered a few females that she considered to be clean, and they began carrying platters and bowls of food out to one of the picnic tables designated for that purpose---platters of buffalo wings, honey barbecue wings, hoagie portions, fried fish, watermelon slices, bowls of chicken salad, salad, chili and Ms. Ruby's potato salad. Ms. Ruby's potato salad was the only potato salad everyone in the neighborhood felt comfortable eating, not to mention it was delicious.

"Hey! Des! I think everybody ready for some music!" Pam yelled to the disc jockey she had hired. D. J. Des nodded his head and put on his headphones---the pint-size disc jockey had setup shop in the middle of the backyard. The lawn was crowded with females and sprinkled with corner boys and ruffians.

When the sounds Tyler *The* Creator's "*Wusyaname*" engulfed all in attendance the vibe was harmonious. The females, some scantily clad and all dressed to impress, sang along loudly---word for word. Locs, kinky-twists, wet and wavy and Indonesian jet-black #9, shook frantically with the music. Even a few grandmothers attending the cookout sang along, as did the children.

Gracie was shoveling hamburger patties and frankfurters onto the foiled grill as quickly as she could. While some of the hooligans huddled around the ice-filled tub that held a variety of beer.

Annette came out of the house with an armful of red plastic cups that contained blended liquors. She handed one to Pam, then the rest to the mature women. Pam took a gulp from her cup then waved her half-empty cup over her head as she danced.

Suddenly the disc jockey's sound system was drowned out by the roar of the luxury sportscar's engine that came from the front of the house. A few of the females, all too familiar with the roaring hurried to the front of Pam's house where Ralph sat *stunting* in his fire engine red Dodge Challenger SRT Hellcat with the always-noticeable obsidian hood.

Pam's cookouts were the equivalent of the NBA's All-Star Weekend, so the *d-boys*, hustlers, hooligans, and femme fatales spared no expense---extravagance was a must. Everyone wanted to be seen, recognized, and remembered for those seven or eight hours. Ralph was no exception he had parked the magnificent machine on the front lawn, sideways. Quickly hopping out, giving the paper chasing females only a glimpse of the soft-looking beige leather interior. They swarmed him as he brushed imaginary linty from his brilliant white Amiri three-button polo-style shirt and jeans. The sun adding more sparkle to his jewelry---a pawnshop-purchased rose gold Rolex watch, a diamond chain and white and black Givenchy sneakers.

A few of the *corner boys* looked at him as inspiration and motivation, the females looked at him as a *sponsor* and potential baby-daddy. While the ruffians looked at him as an easy come up.

Ralph ambled towards the back of the house as D.J. Des began spinning Money Mu's *"Hittin'"*. He greeted Pam with a hug and a kiss on the cheek.

"Damn, Ralph! Life must be *treatin'* you good---you getting all fat in the face," Pam exclaimed as she caressed his golden-brown cheeks in her manicured hands.

"It's *treatin'* me pretty good," he answered with a smile. It was the dope boy way, get money and eat good. Ralph was eating really good. He just hoped that Pam noticed---he had had a crush on her for years and he had heard the rumors that she was attracted to younger men. And he was young at just nineteen.

"Go *an'* get you a plate and *somethin'* to drink---the burgers ain't quite done, but it's some wings an' sandwiches over there," she said pointing in the direction of the picnic table. "And comeback."

*She is flirting,* Ralph thought as he walked over to the table. The D. J. mixed in the latest Lil' Baby song and the females went crazy. Ralph found himself surrounded by asses and elbows.

· · · · · · · · · · · · · · · · · · · · · · · · · · · · · · · · · · · · · · · · · · · · · · · · · · · · · · · · · · · · · · · · · · · · · · · · · · · · · ·

Hot Shot and Yami were experiencing major adrenaline rushes as they watched the canine clashes that took place behind the dilapidated yellow house on Icemorelee Street. The fawn-colored Pitbull Terrier was gnawing viciously at the neck of a solid-black Pitbull---the black purebred bitch bawling in pain as she was shaken and tossed around.

"*Dhat's dhat* bullshit!" Hot Shot vented as he slapped twenty dollars into the hand of the opposing bettor. Aware that the solid-black canine had been defeated.

"You ready to go?" Hot Shot asked as he turned to his friend---he already knew Yami's answer.

"Yeah." Yami was already walking to the car, saying his goodbyes as he did so.

"Ay, CP---*I'ma* holla at you. Ya'll be easy," Hot Shot said as he made his was around to the passenger side. "Trav', next time we bet five *hunned* or better!"

"We can bet one more right now, real quick," the freckle-faced hooligan announced.

"Nah---I gotta go," Hot Shot said as he climbed into the *donk* and slammed the door. Yami had the vehicle in motion before he could reconsider the wager.

Yami had one thing on his mind---Pam. He had a feeling he had enjoyed Monroe much more than Charlotte. He turned up the car stereo and they blasted Denzel Curry all the way to the Southside.

• • • • • • • • • • • • • • • • • • • • • • • • • • • • • • • • • • • • • • • • •

"What the fuck?!" Hot Shot exclaimed as they slowly drove up to Pam's house. The streets were packed---females sashayed to and from the house, scurrying from the ruffians that grabbed at their asses. Kids played tag, squirted each other with water guns and danced to the music.

"They out this *muthaphukka*," Yami uttered as he continued to drive slowly through the masses. Being mindful of the children who occasionally ran into the streets as his eyes roamed from one curvaceous female to the next.

"What the fuck?!" Hot Shot continued.

"Where she at? Who you see?!" Yami quizzed, trying to see who it was that had his friend excited.

"Them rides! Muthaphukkaz got Hellcats and Mustangs sittin' in the yard!"

Not only was Ralph's Hellcat parked in Pam's yard, but it was now accompanied by a black-on-black hardtop late model Porsche Carrera GT with 19-inch lip rims accentuating Pirelli tires. It was blocked in by the Porsche, and the d-boy sitting on the Porsche surrounded by *sponsor-seekers* looked familiar to Hot Shot.

"Park yo' shit in the yard!" Hot Shot ordered as he continued to stare at the dope boy---recognition tickling his brain. Whoever he was he was doing it big, no question. As soon as Yami had the *donk* parked Hot Shot maneuvered out. Once he touched the ground, he was caught off guard by the ruckus the young hustler created as he came off the Porsche.

"Oh! Shit! My nigga, Hot Shot! I heard you was home, but you been on the low. Oh, shit!"

Hot Shot looked at the dope boy---his dark-skinned frame fashioned in even darker fabrics, but they were just as flamboyant as the jewels on his neck. He wore a Gucci Jacquard Hawaiian shirt and short set with matching flip-flops.

Hot Shot could not take his eyes off the awkward looking d-boy's white gold and black diamond encrusted Jesus piece. It was the kind of charm and chain he had saw on the necks of rap stars shopping in Iceboxx videos, the kind that rappers spent their whole advance on.

"Yeah, I ah---been home a minute. Stayin' low-key," Hot Shot said as he excepted the hand extended to him. Still unable to put a name with the face.

"It's me! Ball!" The young d-boy said, realizing that Hot Shot did not recognize him. "I was at Laquesha's house one time when you called---I gave her fifty dollars to put on your books."

"Oh, okay---what's good?!" Hot Shot said as he embraced the hustler, recalling the event. He tried to remember anything involving money. "Ball---I remember you now. Niggaz was sayin' you was *pushin'* a cocaine white Lexus convertible when I was in prison."

"Yeah, the ISC 350---I was. I traded it in for the Porsche," Ball said nonchalantly as he pointed over his shoulder towards the sports car.

"Dhat's what up. But who *pushin'* the Hellcat?"

Ball looked at Hot Shot with disdain. "That bitch-ass nigga Ralph. That lame ain't even from the Southside, but he be over this muthaphukka like *er'day*," Ball answered dryly.

"Ralph from Camp Sutton?" Hot Shot asked, rubbing his chin. Yami just listened closely, saying nothing.

"Yeah, that fool."

"Ralph dhat move weight? Keep getting' robbed?"

"Yeah," Ball exclaimed with aversion. "That nigga."

"Damn, nigga doin' good, ain't he?" Hot Shot said as he looked at Yami for confirmation. "Nigga pushin' a new Hellcat."

"It's an '16, though." Ball blurted enviously.

'Ain't dhat Porsche you got an '05?" Yami asked.

"Yeah, but, ah---I had my shit first," Ball explained as if what he said was making sense. "That nigga's a fraud. Watch though---I'ma get the new Jag' as soon as the feds cool off 'round here."

"Ball!" A succulent honey-brown female with braces in a green tube-top, pink Lycra shorts and canvas Vans beckoned as she stood with a super thick white girl and an obese, chocolate-complected female who held a camera. "Come take a picture with us next to your car."

"I need to *holla* at you *'bout somethin'*---hold up for a sec'," Ball said, excusing himself.

"These young boys out here *gettin'* it. I remember when dhat lil' nigga was running back and forth to the store for the dope boys dhat was getting it when I left the streets---movin' lil' half, quarters an' shit," Hot Shot informed Yami, never taking his eyes off the jackleg photo shoot. He was captivated by the white girl's curves and what she had stuffed into her skinny jeans.

She noticed him watching and whispered to her honey-brown friend. Honey-brown looked up at Hot Shot with a simper. "Hot Shot--- my girl, Lacey wanna know if you wanna take a picture with us," she said. "Really she wants you to take a picture with her."

"I can do dhat," he answered as he walked over and boldly put his bulging arm around her tan frame. He did not know if it had come from the years of viewing white girls in numerous Curve Magazines, but he was filled with lust. Lacy knew of this lust because of the stiff dick against her ass. She looked back over her shoulder and smiled, fingering her blonde hair behind her ear.

"Kim---you and Ball step out the way, let me get dem real quick," the obese female instructed, aiming the camera as if she was a professional photographer. Ball and his sorority-cutie home from Johnson C. Smith University moved aside.

"Hold up!" Ball yelled as he rushed the couple. "Flash a stack on 'em." He handed Hot Shot a stack of fifty-dollar bills constrained by rubber bands which he eagerly accepted. The photographer snapped photo after photo---allowing them to change poses.

Lacy became comfortable behind Hot Shot with her hands on his pectorals. She even convinced him to take off his wife-beater---her hands roamed his chest and rock-hard abs.

"Lacy! Stop being nasty!" Kim shouted, teasing her friend. Lacy blushed as Hot Shot whispered in her ear

"Damn, a nigga go to prison an' the first thing he do when he get home is get a bitch!" LaLa said dryly as she sauntered up in a hugged her white windbreaker with plum trim and white short shorts that hugged her hips and ass. Her calves decorated and accentuated with gold lace-up Dolce and Gabbana stiletto heels. Her hair was an *unbeweavable* plum and white lace-front, which oddly complemented her yellow skin tone.

Dejanee and Alexis stood behind their friend shaking their heads giving Hot Shot cross looks. When LaLa sashayed towards the backward with one of the *nastiest* walks Hot Shot had ever seen. Dejanee and Alexis did their best to imitate it as the followed close behind LaLa.

Hot Shot was disgusted with himself. "Hey, who the fuck was dhat?" Yami asked.

"LaLa," Hot Shot said with a frown. He looked at Lacy. "I'ma get back up *wit'* you, a'ight?"

She shrugged her shoulders and turned to her friend Kim giving her a *what's going on* expression.

"Hey, LaLa thicker than duck butter my nig'!" Yami exclaimed as he grabbed himself suggestively, following Hot Shot as he tried to catch up with the female of his desire.

LaLa was quite thick---voluptuous. More voluptuous than she had been when Hot Shot went away to prison. She teased the tape measure with her 34B-28-46 measurements. Hot Shot stood behind her five-six frame almost stalkerish as she chatted with a group of females. He could not take his eyes off her.

D. J. Des began playing a southern favorite---every female, every child and only a handful of the ruffians began dancing. Doing everything from the *Renegade* to the *Up* as they sang the infectious lyrics to Cardi B's "Up".

Hot Shot and Yami watched LaLa and her retinue *Oui*-ed and *Laffy-Taffy remixed* as a shirtless ruffian dirty flexed during their cipher. LaLa slung hips and ass like a *dope boy* slung crack on payday.

Ralph attempted to walk by the group with his plate of wings, but LaLa quickly snatched him close---Alexis relieved him of his plate of wings, continuing to bounce to the beat as she scarfed down buffalo wings. LaLa grinded on the young hustler with passion as the disc jockey mixed in a vintage track---Mad Cobra's "Flex." The backyard barbecue became raunchy.

Dejanee could see that Hot Shot was fuming so she swiftly went over to him, threw her arms around his huge nek and began grinding on him---summoning for Yami with her index finger. He crept up behind her and began grinding on her big bulging ass that was barely concealed by the electric blue Shein-bought dress she wore.

Hot Shot found himself struggling to keep up with Dejanee's sensually erratic rhythm having been gone away for some time and being out of touch with the latest dances. He nonchalantly eased away, but before he could make it to the table covered with food, Alexis was on him---feeding him wings and dancing suggestively in her hot pink baby tee, her dark, distressed denim short-shorts and the tiniest pair of hot pink #3 Jordans that the convict had ever seen.

Yami had his lanky arms wrapped snugly around Dejanee's mahogany-complected frame as they danced. She smiled gleefully, her dimples on display as her dark brown eyes focused on Hot Shot.

"Why you so stuck on LaLa? She fuckin' with Ball---get over it. He's a dope boy, that's what she like. Get your money up," Alexis said dryly as she turned to grind her massive ass on him. D. J. Des spun Megan Thee Stallion's "Thot Shit". All of the gyrating and ass jiggling had Hot Shot horny---he wanted to fuck.

"'Cuse me---bitch!" Pam blurted as she rolled her eyes and snatched Yami away from his dance partner. Dejanee looked on in awe as Pam slightly staggering led Yami into the house---LaLa laughed, as did other onlookers.

"We need to talk," Pam announced once she had Yami inside. "Ya'll excuse us."

She led Yami back towards her bedroom, away from the crowded kitchen---once they were inside her bedroom Pam closed the door and pushed him onto the plush queen-size bed. He looked up to her bewildered, pulling his dreads away from his face.

"Look, Yami---I don't know what type of bitches you used to fuckin' wit', but I thought I made it clear to you when we first met what it was," Pam said as she straddled his waist and began undoing his belt---staring down at down at him like a famished feline about to devour her prey.

"Naw, I 'on't *thaink* you made *yo'self* clear. Show me what you talkin' 'bout," Yami said in a low guttural tone as his hands grasped her haunches. His fingertips roguishly caressing the warm caramel flesh of her derriere.

Pam urgently unfastened his Dickie shorts and relieved him of his shirt---kissing his small, chiseled chest ravenously as he fumbled with the zipper on her short-shorts. Once Yami had her shorts undone he tossed her to the side and aggressively removed them, along with her white thong. Pam was already stroking his long black dick in her petite hand, priming his manhood with an inviting look on her face.

Yami stood over her, his dick now rock hard and ready---and Pam just knew he was going to slide in between her thighs and stretch her warm, wet insides, but he had other plans. He flipped her over so that she was on her hands and knees, her pretty round brown up in the air---before Pam could take satisfaction in his strength, Yami pushed down on the small of her back, burying her face in one of the down-filled pillows as he buried his manhood deep inside her pussy.

Pam's screams were muffled by the pillow as Yami punished her pussy---thrusting like a madman as he gave her all nine veined and pulsating inches of himself. Pam's fingernails dug into the comforter as she tried to pull away from her ruffian-lover. Yami grunted as he continued to assault her womb---in and out, in and out. His nuts slapping against her pussy loudly.

"*Ooooh! Ye-eah!* Right there!" Pam yelled, managing to free her face from the pillow.

"Ahh shit," Yami groaned as he came, doubling over from the powerfully erotic sensation. "Pussy *gooder* than a muthaphukka."

She was not even disappointed---she was quite pleased with his eight-minute performance. Her body trembled as he slowly eased out of her. Pam felt like sucking her thumb and playing with her earlobe, the sex had been that soothing. No tender lovemaking, just rough and raw passion. That is exactly what she had needed---a good fucking.

Yami quickly dressed, kissed Pam on her big, beautiful ass, then left her alone in her bedroom with her disheveled hairdo, her thoughts and a warm puddle of his love nectar which oozed out of her womanhood onto her thigh.

*********************************************

As soon as Yami stepped onto the lawn he was bombarded by Dejanee. "That's how you do me?" She asked pouting her glossy lips. "Ms. Pam your *ol' lady* now?"

Yami found her sarcasm and jealously amusing. "It ain't even like that."

"It's like somethin'---ya'll was in there doin' somethin'. You come out *wit'* sweat all on your forehead," she said dryly. Yami could see she was playing detective and was not about to let up. D.J. Des was a life-saver---he began playing French Montana's "Unforgettable".

"You wanna dance?" Yami asked.

"Yeah." And just like that, all was forgotten---Dejanee was bent over with her electric blue dress hiked up almost to her waist, her black G-string visible and pressed against Yami's crotch as she oscillated her plump ass.

Hot Shot sat at one picnic tables greedily eating a burger and wings as he listened intently to Ball as he vented his hatred and jealously. "I'm tellin' you. That nigga soft as fuck---runnin' 'round here like he got it! He got it, but he ain't got more than me," Ball ranted. "I know how you get down, Hot Shot. I used to see you *layin'* hustlers down back in the day. I'll pay you to get that nigga---just because I don't wanna see him *wit' nothin'*. Straight like that! And what I'ma give you is *nothin'* compared to what you'll get off the clown."

"I'll give you five stacks just to rob him an' shoot him in his leg or somethin'," Ball was now whispering. "And I think I know where the nigga stash house is. I got a friend *checkin'* on that."

Hot Shot just nodded and chewed, intrigued by the information that the *d-boy* shared. He was more intrigued by what hatred could force a man to do----get another man up to be *jacked*. Although Hot Shot was focused on what Ball was saying, he kept one eye on Yami and the other on LaLa and Ralph. It was in that split-second that he blinked, and all hell broke loose.

"Bitch! I'ma beat *yo'* ass!" Pam yelled as she rushed Dejanee with a flurry of fists. Dejanee did her best to defend herself as Yami stepped aside, doing nothing to stop the bout.

Dejanee had her head down and her fists flailing in a windmill-motion. Pam was talking to the young female as she landed punches. "Bitch-I'ma-teach-yo' ass- 'bout-fuckin' wit'-other-bitches-men!"

"Pam!" Gracie shouted in a motherly manner. "The *chil'* wasn't doing nothin' but dancing with the boy. If you going to be actin' like that you don't need to be drinkin'! Somebody break the shit up!"

A few of the corner boys adhering to the command ran over and broke the fight up. Annette sat at the Spades table shaking her head with disgust.

"Ay, I think your man good by himself. Let him know me *an'* you *gon'* go for a ride in the Hellcat," Ball instructed. Trying to regain Hot Shot's attention and convince him that robbing Ralph would be a power move. "You ever ride in a Hellcat?"

"Nah," Hot Shot answered as he got up from the picnic table. He was excited, but he did not want to come off like a giddy hood chick. As he walked over to Yami he noticed the white girl from earlier shaking her rotund derriere and looking at him. He smiled and nodded in her direction---not paying attention to where he was walking.

"Excuse you!" LaLa yelled. A frown and a look of pain on her face as she pushed Hot Shot off her foot. "If you would keep your nose all out dhat white bitch ass you could watch where you walkin'!"

"Hold up," the convict said coolly, grabbing her by the wrists. "I apologize, but you ain't gotta come at me all salty like *dhat*. I ain't did shit to you---I'm tryna get at you, real talk. What's *to* you?"

"Let me go, Hot Shot." She said as she snatched away from his grasp. "You ain't tryin' to get at nobody but *dhat* white bitch---if you was you would get yo' shit together, get your stacks up. A bitch need *thangs*."

LaLa was looking into his eyes, hoping she got her point across. But Hot Shot did not see a sense of urgency, he saw greed---a lust for the almighty dollar. The same lust he, himself had for the dollar, because he knew it was what he needed to possess her.

"Move, Hot Shot," she said with a pout as she exhaled exasperatedly. LaLa pushed on his chest, but here effort was minimal, allowing her hands to linger on his massive chest. "I gotta go check on my girl, she got muthaphukkaz putting they hands on her an' shit! Dhat sit ain't cool."

· · · · · · · · · · · · · · · · · · · · · · · · · · · · · · · · · · · · · · · · · · · · · · · · · · · · · · · ·

"Slow the fuck down! Shit!" Hot Shot screamed from the passenger seat of the Porsche GT. He felt nauseous. Ball was maneuvering the sportscar at 121mph through a section of Maurice

Street known only as Seven Hills---a rollercoaster ride of pavement that was appropriately titled. A landscape to be reckoned with.

Ball laughed loudly as Dave East's "Handsome" blared from the state-of-the-art sound system. Then he brought the black Porsche to an abrupt halt at the intersecting streets of Maurice and Sunset. Just when Hot Shot's stomach was settling the dope boy signaled right and turned with the gas pedal to the floor as he shifted gears and came off the brake.

"I love this shit!" Ball yelled before slowing the sportscar down and turning into the lot of a gas station where he parked and turned off the radio.

"This'll be the first an' last time I ever ride *wit' yo'* ass, Rad Racer," Hot Shot said with a chuckle as he regained his composure.

"*Sheeeeit*, this car will probably be how I die---*speedin'*," the young d-boy said. As if prophesying his own death. Hot Shot could tell by the expression on his face that Ball was dead serious.

"Well don't let me be in this muthaphukka wit' you when you go. And what's up wit' what we was talking about? Your boy, Ralph an' dhat stash house?"

"Word is---he fuckin with the Mexican muthaphukka Erica used to fuck wit'---God bless the dead. Anyway---the *muthaphukka* called Taco. Taco *frontin'* the nigga like five or six birds at a time."

"Why don't I just lay Taco down?" Hot Shot asked with a quizzical expression.

"Nah," Ball said nervously as he shook his head. "You don't wanna do that---that nigga MS, Mexican Mafia, or somethin'. Nah, you don't wanna do that."

Hot Shot understood the warning very clearly.

'Five or six *birds*---what? He *coppin'* like *dhat* every month?"

Ball exhaled, staring out the window as he spoke. "Nah, but I will be and that's real talk. I*'ma* be *runnin'* this muthaphukka," he said matter-of-factly.

"I feel you," Hot Shot said nodding his head in agreement.

'Look---it's around this time that he usually re-up, so it might be like four birds in the spot---he move that shit in weight. Quarter, halves, shit like that. It's money in the spot---niggaz say a *hunned thou'* or better. I don't see it."

"What you see?" Hot Shot asked---laughing on the inside at the hater.

"Maybe ninety stacks,' Ball said scratching his head.

The nerve of this little muthafukka," Hot Shot thought to himself.

"Ain't nothin' else to talk about--- you get me the location to dhat stash house an' who up in there and I'll handle my part, you just keep your mouth shut."

"I got you," Ball said tapping his hand to his heart then to his lips. Then from out of nowhere he pulled a Glock26 and handed it to Hot Shot. "I want you to shoot him wit' my shit."

"No problem," the ex-con said as he checked to make sure the safety was on before stuffing the gun into the waistband of his jeans. "My money?"

"Oh, I got you," Ball said with a smirk as he pulled a dual-banded stack from his pocket and tossed it in Hot Shop's lap. "You ain't gotta count it, it's all there."

"Shit me," Hot Shot snorted as he began counting the stack of money. "Niggaz wit' GEDs miscount money, too."

Ball laughed as he put the Porsche in gear and exited the lot.

● ● ● ● ● ● ● ● ● ● ● ● ● ● ● ● ● ● ● ● ● ● ● ● ● ● ● ● ● ● ● ● ● ● ● ● ● ● ● ● ● ● ● ● ● ● ● ● ● ● ● ● ● ● ● ● ●

"Look, Dejanee---you ain't gotta leave. I said I was sorry for *puttin'* my hands on you. I was wrong. I been drinkin'---maybe too much," Pam explained as all in attendance looked on, those that gave a damn.

"Ms. Pam, I thought we was better than dhat---but I guess I thought wrong." Dejanee said dryly as she pointed her finger accusingly.

"Ain't nobody get hurt. Why you just *cain't* let shit go?!" Pam insisted.

"Bitch! You snatched some of my tracks out!" Dejanee shouted as she held up pink pieces of hair weave as evidence.

"What you ain't getting' ready to do is stand in my yard an' call me out my name! Now---I was trying to be nice and apologize to yo' ass, but I see I'm 'bout to have to beat the shit out you again!" Pam had a hand on her hip and the other waving recklessly in Dejanee's face--- Pam's neck and head wriggled as she spoke.

Dejanee rolled her eyes, smacked her lips and shifted her weight from one foot to the other as she looked off at nothing---Pam continued to rant. "Let me tell you somethin'---

*WHAM!* Dejanee caught Pam with a left hook---staggering her. *WHAM!* Another left hand connected with Pam's face, but it was the last. Annette, Pam and Gracie with a metal spatula began assaulting Dejanee as if she was L.A. riot victim.

It was total chaos when Ball and Hot Shot arrived back at the house. Disc Jockey Des was on the microphone trying to bring order to the out-of-control situation and protect his equipment at the same time.

It appeared that everyone was participating in a violent game of human tug-of-war---there was a group on one side trying to pull Dejanee apart from Pam. Dejanee had Pam by her leg and what was left of her camisole. Pam had her by her hair, her real hair---her real hair and her skimpy attire which now resembled a cloth belt---she nearly naked.

LaLa and Alexis were crammed into the group trying to maintain a hold on Dejanee as titties and ass shook loosely for all to see. Some of the *corner boys* pretending to break up the ruckus just to cop feels on both Pam and Dejanee.

Hot Shot did the most sensible, yet the most erratic and dangerous thing anyone could do during a hood brawl. ***Blammmm!*** He fired a round from the Glock 26 into the air---everyone dispersed, everyone but Pam and Dejanee. They stood breathing hard and gazing at each other menacingly.

"What the fuck wrong with ya'll?!" Hot Shot chastised. "We all *s'pose* to be out here *enjoyin'* ourselves! I mean---I'd like to see both of *ya'll* ass-naked, but not like this. Chill the fuck out!"

His eyes went from one half-naked female to the other. Yami laughed at his partner's comments as he walked over---a *choppa* with a drum magazine in his right hand at his side. A *choppa* as it was affectionately called in the hood in this case was an AK-47 assault rifle of any brand. "You a fool my nig'," he interjected.

"Ain't shit funny, Yami! You started all this shit," Pam said matter-of-factly as she rolled her eyes at the ruffian.

"Go *'head wit' dhat* shit shone---I ain't get shit started," Yami insisted with false irritation. His lust now awakened as his eyes went from Pam's curvaceous body to Dejanee's young succulent body.

"You did, Yami! You think you got it like that—you got two bitches out here *fightin'* over *yo'* sorry ass! You ain't got it like that!" Dejanee screamed in his face before sauntering away.

Pam just stared up at Yami with those seductive slanted eyes--- unable to fix her lips to say the words her young opposition had. What Yami had he enjoyed and didn't want to lose it. He just had to work on his staying power.

"Yami---we *gotta* go." Hot Shot announced. Yami looked at the ex-con, trying to read his facial expression. He was unable to, so without another word they headed towards the *donk*. Yami put the *choppa* back in the trunk and climbed into the vehicle and they drove away.

∎∎∎∎∎∎∎∎∎∎∎∎∎∎∎∎∎∎∎∎∎∎∎∎∎∎∎∎∎∎∎∎∎∎∎∎∎∎∎∎∎∎∎∎∎∎∎∎∎∎∎∎∎

Dejanee stood at the sink in front of the mirror while LaLa and Alexis stood in the doorway watching their friend examine herself.

"Dat bitch ain't gotta worry 'bout me comin' to no more of her cookouts," LaLa said dryly as she shook her head, dissatisfied by the day's events.

"Me either," Alexis added unconvincingly.

"Fuck that ol' ass bitch," Dejanee said vehemently as she pressed lightly on the small lump under her left eye. "It ain't over."

"Let it go," Alexis said pursuing her lips.

"She's right---let it go." LaLa added.

Yami and Hot Shot were sitting on porch of Hot Shot's aunt's apartment smoking a blunt when Ball pulled to the curb in his black Porsche. It was just after six-thirty and the sun was still beaming---both ruffians quickly got off the porch and trotted to the sportscar.

"Ay, what's up?" Ball said as he turned down the car stereo---the sounds of Trouble's "Kesha Dem" was still audible. "I got that info for you."

"Where it's at?" Hot Shot's tone was aggressive.

"The nigga got a stash house on Walk-up Avenue. It's a brick crib with light blue trim---2999. It's some lil' ex-smoker chick he be fuckin' wit' crib---her name Latrice or somethin' like that. But you ain't gotta worry about her, she at the fish tables. It's gon' be two big *niggaz* up in there---Monster and Big Will," Ball explained as he sipped the codeine cocktail in the red plastic cup he held. "Now his crib is on the next street over, he stay cliqued-up when he at home, jack boys done ran up in his shit like three times. He gon' be back and forth---you just get him at the stash house, that's where the money at."

"Dhat's what's up," Hot Shot said, his arms folded as he rubbed his chin. Yami shook his head in agreement and took a toke from the blunt in his hand.

"I would ask you if you need a piece my man, but I saw what you strapped wit'---that *stick*," Ball said with laughter. He loved the mentality of a real street nigga---always strapped. "I'ma let you gentlemen handle yo' business."

Dap was exchanged between the three, then Ball drove off and Hot Shot and Yami were in the Chevy on their way to Ralph's stash house.

Coincidentally, when Yami brought the *donk* to a halt at the intersection and signaled right---Ralph slowly cruised by in his '79 cottonwood green Cadillac, which had undergone a drastic hood makeover. Hot Shot and Yami were seeing it for the first time, but the Cadillac's top had been chopped and everything had once been chrome was now gold-dipped, even the *elbows*.

All three men made eye contact---predators and prey as the Tee Grizzley & Lil' Durk's "3rd Person" came from the old school Cadillac competed with 2 Chainz's "Hot Wings" which came thundering from the trunk of the classic Chevy.

"Go straight! Go straight!" Hot Shot exclaimed as he tried to appear composed. "Dhat was that nigga right there. We don't want the nigga to think we following him---he fuck around an' get nervous he might never go to the stash. They say the nigga scary like dhat."

Despite his right signal still flickering, Yami kept straight when the light changed green. "Dhat young nigga got it don't he? A 'lac and a Hellcat! I heard some *shones* at the cookout talkin' 'bout he got a bike, too. Ninja ABS with the crazy light system." Yami informed his partner-in-crime. It was evident from Yami's tone that he was eager to leave the young hustler's pockets hurting.

Yami turned right onto Highway 74, drove past the KFC then made a left onto Walkup Avenue---the Chevy moved at a slow creep as it passed one affordable domicile after another.

"There go the *'lac*---right there!" Hot Shot announced as he pointed to the Cadillac and the blue-trimmed house it was parked beside. His blood pumping through his veins erratically as adrenaline surged through his body---intensifying his marijuana high. "Pull into *dhat* driveway where them Mexican kids *playin'* at."

Yami parked three houses down from where Ralph was parked. The young *chicanos* with their mongrel of a dog watched the two black men cautiously as they exited the extravagantly painted car---the tall, dark-skinned, long-haired thug retrieving an assault rifle from the trunk before the two swiftly disappeared behind the neighbor's house. The boys resumed playing as the day slowly faded into night as if they had seen nothing unusual.

Hot Shot and Yami having quickly made their way to Ralph's stash house where they plastered themselves against the vinyl siding, anxiously awaiting to make their next move. The fact that the stash house had no backdoor, but instead a side door, slightly complicated things.

"My nigga---we gotta get up in this muthaphukka quick---get out even quicker. You hear me?" Hot Shot whispered as he searched Yami's eyes for any sign of fear---there was none. "It's lights out for these niggaz, you hear me?"

Yami knew exactly what his cohort meant.

"*Lissen*---I'ma kick the door," Hot Shot explained as he watched Yami's expression change. "We shoot last 'cause we don't know where shit at---we shoot ast, if we can help it. Oh, an' fuck you nigga."

"What?" Yami chuckled lightly.

"I *seen yo'* face when I said I was gon' kick in the door. Don't let these lil' legs fool you," Hot Shot said with low laughter---referring to his own penitentiary build. Massive upper body and little legs, and his partner's doubt about him kicking in the door.

"Remember what I said---you can hurt a muthaphukka, but we need to know where the stash at first, befo' we put they lights out. You ready?"

Hot Shot did not wait for an answer, he had his gun out and was moving urgently to the side of the house. Yami was close behind, the AK-47 gripped with both hands. Hot Shot kicked the door with monstrous force, it was not enough. The second kick took the door off the hinges and the two ruffians were in the kitchen, guns drawn, watching a startled Ralph struggle to get his pants up---a half-naked, ebony-complected female bent over the sink with a look of horror on her face. Only one leg was confined jeans her skinny jeans, the other was exposed---succulent and youthful. Unlike her face which was still pretty but was aged by years of smoking crack-cocaine.

It was undoubtedly that the female was Latrice---Ball's information was inaccurate. Her huge breasts heaving rapidly beneath her micro boy-beater with each frightened breath hung awkwardly from her five-two, one hundred- and thirteen-pound frame. The once dope-fed vixen's measurements were 34F-24-34. She made no attempt to dress--- she was frozen with fear.

The television in the living room blared rap music, no question the location of Ralph's hired goons. Ralph made an idiotic attempt to reach for the pistol on the kitchen table just behind him. Yami let loose with the *stick*---***Phop! Phop! Phop!*** A three round burst crippled the young hustler and forced him to the linoleum floor screaming.

Hot Shot looked at Ralph, studied his wounds quickly and was pleased---Yami had took heed to his words. Of course, Ralph would probably need the assistance of a cane for the rest of his life but fuck it. It was all a part of the dope game.

A rumbling came from the living room---it was Ralph's two humongous goons. One entered the kitchen wielding a sawed-off double-barreled shotgun that he never got the chance to use---two rounds from the Glock 26 opened his skull and he collapsed, face down, or rather what was left of his face. The other goon looked at life differently and dropped his chrome pistol. "Man, I *'on't* want no problems *wit'* you niggaz! I promise," he pleaded as he fell to his knees.

Ralph looked at his hired help with disgust as he, himself cowered on the floor whimpering. Hot Shot, too, was disgusted with the goon's *bitchassness.* He wanted to beat the shit out of him, but first the hustler had to sees just what his dope money had bought him---a coward who would fold at first sight of bloodshed.

Hot Shot stormed over to the goon and began pistol-whipping him maliciously, each blow drawing blood and exposing pinkish-white flesh. Yami noticed the urine streaming down Latrice's thighs onto the linoleum.

"A'ight---where it at, nigga?!" Hot Shot was already eyeing the quarter-key of hard that was on display on the kitchen table, drying in front of a battery-operated mini fan. Along with three rubber-banded stacks---five thousand dollars in each stack in assorted bills.

"It's right there on the table, playboy." Ralph groaned. He knew Hot Shot's legend and did not want to upset or insult the *jackboy*, but he had---all because he did not want to part with what was his. "It's yours."

"Muthaphukka--- you tryna play me!" Hot Shot was on Ralph before he could blink twice---stomping his already shattered bullet-riddled kneecap and shin as he screamed for mercy.

"It's all right there, man I swear!" Ralph cried out as the bulky ruffian continued to stomp him. Latrice could hear the violence, she did not need to see it---she was now clutching the sink, shaking uncontrollably.

Yami walked over to the former fiend and slowly ran his hand over her right breast to her bare ass. Then from there his hand found his way to her moist pussy, allowing his fingers to part her pussy lips. "Me an' my man got dhat thang wet," he whispered into her ear as he continued fondling her. The AK-47 still braced in his right hand. "Look here, shone---if you got any kind of love for dhat nigga an' don't want him to get killed, you'll tell me where the stash at."

Latrice began crying as she contemplated her dilemma---say nothing and witness Ralph's demise, and possibly her own. Or tell the *jack boys* where everything was and reduce Ralph's empire tremendously. This could mean losing everything she strived for---committing herself to rehab, because Ralph had promised her a better life if she did so. Her home, and her daughter in DSS custody who she sought to regain in just a few months---all of this she sought to lose. Ralph's screams pulled her back from her thoughts.

"Don't hurt him. I'll get you the stuff---the money, the dope, whatever. Just don't hurt him," she muttered. Yami smiled---satisfied.

"Be easy my nig'---the *shone gon'* act right," Yami informed Hot Shot who still administering a beating to the young hustler.

"Go get *dhat*," Hot Shot demanded. Yami pulled his fingers from Latrice's womanhood, sniffed them, then nudged her away from the sink. She stumbled forward as she tried to dress. Yami smacked her on her naked ass which caused her to fall.

"Get yo' ass up *an'* let's get it!" Yami yelled, his look now threatening. Latrice quickly put her jeans on properly and stood. "Let's get it!"

She cautiously stepped over the dead goon's body, nervously peering over her shoulder ever few seconds, fearing she would receive a bullet to the back of her head as she led the *jack boy* to the small hallway closet. There she removed two large vacuums.

"What's this?" Yami asked with a puzzled look. Latrice kneeled, unzipped the bag compartment of one vacuum and began removing kilo after kilo of cocaine until the bag was empty. The jack boy looked at the five kilos insatiately---Latrice had her hand inside the other vacuum removing stack after stack of cash. It was as if she had never stop.

"Ay, when you get all dhat out---put it in one of them pillowcases," Yami instructed as he pointed to the bed linen on the middle shelf of the closest. Latrice sniffed and cried as she followed his orders, then handed up the loot-filled pillowcase.

They say a woman's intuition is keen, so astute that Latrice closed her eyes. ***Phop! Phop! Phop!*** The spent casings clanged to the hardwood floor. "You shouldna been here, shawty," Yami muttered apathetically as he walked back to the kitchen.

"It ain't gotta be like this, real talk. I ain't gon' say nothin'," the so-called goon was saying as Yami entered the kitchen.

"Shut the fuck up---Pussy!" Yami shouted as he kicked the cowardly security. Without another word or warning the *jack boy* squeezed the trigger. ***Phop! Phop! Phop! Phop! Phop! Phop!***

Hot Shot sat Ralph in a chair with one hand. "Dhat shit on yo' neck an' wrist, run dhat, nigga," he said through clenched teeth. Ralph slowly removed his jewelry and placed it in the ex-con's waiting hand.

Ralph could not even look up at Hot Shot. He lowered his head and put his hands in his lap. Hot Shot pressed the barrel of the Glock 26 against the hustler's skull and fired two rounds---Ralph was dead before his body hit the floor.

"Let's roll!" Hot Shot yelled to his crime partner. The gunshots had rendered him deaf for the moment. They exited the house to find it completely dark out---running to Yami's car.

······················································································

Back at Hot Shot's aunt's apartment, Hot Shot and Yami were held up in his bedroom--- listening to Lil' Baby and smoking blunts while Hot Shot counted the money on the floor of the tin room. Yami sat on the dresser peeking out the window and toying with the Glock---it was dark out and the temperature was still hot.

"Hey! Where you say yo' aunt was at?" Yami asked as Hot Shot continued to count money, trying not to miscount the ill-gotten cash.

Hot Shot looked up at his friend with a flustered expression on his face. "She down at 'Laine playin' Tunk for money," he explained--- almost losing count.

"I thought you said yo' man, Ball comin' through."

"He is---he'll be here in about ten minutes," Hot Shot answered as he tried to keep an accurate count. "It ain't what a nigga said we'd get, but it's damn near close."

"How much is it?" Yami asked impatiently---Hot Shot gave him a teasing grin.

"Ain't much."

"How much is *ain't much*?" Yam asked with mocking irritation.

"Eighty-five g's, my nigga!" Hot Shot slapped two stacks of money together excitedly. "You wanna count it?"

"Naw---I trust you my nig'. You like fam'," Yami said assuring as he watched the ex-con begin dividing the money.

"Dhat's what's up. I trust you too."

***BLAM! BLAM! BLAM!*** Hot Shot looked at the three gaping holes in his chest, then up at Yami---his so-called friend and crime partner. He found it extremely hard to catch his breath and even harder to believe he had just been betrayed. But it was what it was---part of the game, as they say.

Hot Shot fell backwards, the stacks of cash he had been counting clutched tightly in his fists as his spirit left his body.

"Good lookin' out my nig'," Yami said as he forced the gun into his waistband and began gathering the money and drugs. "I told *ya* we like fam'---I see you put me I *ya* will an' left me *er'thang*."

Yami's laughter was abruptly interrupted by the roarin g engine of the Porsche outside of the apartment. He knew he had to maintain his composure, pace himself. He had to be calculated.

He was on the Southside, and he knew it was like any other hood in America---you had your nosey people, but people did not always rush to call the police at the sounds of gunshots. They were numb to the violence.

Yami calmly walked through the apartment into the living room, opened the front door and signaled for the young *d-boy* to come in. Ball exited the car and moved suspiciously towards the apartment.

"Ay! What up---where my nigga at?!" Ball asked gleefully as he entered the apartment and closed the door behind himself.

Yami smiled and pointed towards the bedrooms. "He back there---chillin'," he answered as he ushered Ball down the hallway with a hand on his shoulder.

Ball would have gone into shock from the sight of the dead *jackboy* sprawled out on the floor and the hand gripping his shoulder like death, but losing his own life is what he feared. ***BLAM! BLAM!*** The shots to the back of his cranium removed all fear. Shot with his own gun---the gun he had provided and paid for Ralph to be shot with. The irony.

Ball's body dropped to the floor and Yami did not flinch---he was bent over the corpse, relieving the deceased of his jewelry, adding the jewels to what he was already wearing---the jewelry he had pilfered from Ralph.

. . . . . . . . . . . . . . . . . . . . . . . . . . . . . . . . . . . . . . . . . . . . . . . . . . . . . . . . . .

"Ain't nobody seen Yami? Yami?!" Pam yelled as she staggered around her backyard with a bottle of Patron in her hand and not a bruise on her from the brawl---her wardrobe completely different from earlier. Her head now wrapped in a black and grey Gucci scarf to conceal her ruined hairdo. Her thickset frame fashioned in a tight-fitting black v-neck tee, black low-rise skinny jeans and a pair of black and grey Gucci sneakers.

"Hey, Pam," a caramel-complected corner boy blurted as he grabbed her arm to get her attention. "I seen your boy Yami ride in front of Hot Shot's crib. You good/"

Pam stuck her tongue out slow and sensually between her full lips as she stared at the *corner boy's* hand on her arm, then at his face. *Mmm*h, she thought as she gazed at his dimpled-face, fresh cut Ceasar, diamond studs in his ears, tattooed arms and lastly, his immaculate Jordans.

"I'm good," she answered in a flirtatious manner. "I could be better."

"You need anything---holla at y abo," he said with strong confidence. Leaning into her as he continued to hold onto her arm. Pam could smell the faint scent of citrus and musk. This arouse her more than the intricate graffiti that she could now see was carved into his Caesar cut. "Anything."

Pam felt a warmness in her womb as he released her. She knew he could not have been more than nineteen- or twenty-years young, but she wanted him. "Holla," she giggled as she tugged at his belt loop. The cookout, kickback or whatever you wanted to call it was still in full effect---Gracie was still manning the grill, so Pam could slip away unnoticed. "Let's go in the house."

The *corner boy* smiled and followed as she led the way.

••••••••••••••••••••••••••••••••••••••••••••••••••••••••••••••••••••••••••••

Yami was pushing the '87 Chevy well over the speed limit in the dark of night---a large blunt in his mouth, the stereo blasting Yo Gotti's most trending hit and the *choppa* resting on the front seat as he entered Charlotte. The Queen City.

As fate would have it, Charlotte-Mecklenburg Highway Patrol were out on the highways and byways, looking to ticket any and everyone---in a matter of seconds, Yami saw the flashing blue and white lights and heard the siren. He knew he had no choice but to decrease his speed and bring the car to halt on shoulder of Old Charlotte Highway.

Yami sat inside the Chevy draped in stolen jewelry of the deceased, cursing himself for not taking Ball's Porsche as well. He never bothered to turn down the stereo and this irritated Patrolman Yearck when he approached the high-riding Chevy. His eyes level with the driver side window which was tinted to a degree that violated city law.

Yearck, an arrogant rookie with a lopsided crew-cut rapped on the tinted glass loudly with his flashlight, his right-hand hovering over his sidearm. Yami coolly lowered the window releasing the stench of the burning Kush.

The patrolman was immediately assaulted by the rank odor as the beam from the flashlight caught the AK-47 in Yami's hand---a barrage of bullets caught Yearck in the face, neck, and chest, piercing his ballistic vest. The officer danced backwards into oncoming traffic---a trucker's horn blared as the eighteen-wheeler slammed into the lawman. As quickly as it had happened Yami had the *donk* in reverse, wheeling past the patrolman's car and back onto the road, over to the proper lane---continuing to drive in reverse for about a quarter of a mile before spinning the car dangerously onto the highway, pushing the Chevy well over 90 miles per hour as he turned down a backroad that would lead him to Interstate 85. Yami was headed 85 South, his destination Atlanta, Georgia…

## ANOTHER 48

Detective James Berman with his silver head of hair and tanned skinned stood reticently at the crime scene---unmoved by the horrid scene or the stench permeating from the two dead bodies as the heat index reached a tumultuous ninety-nine degrees. He was oblivious of everything and everyone else---the only thing he acknowledged was his crime scene and his victims.

He knelt next to the bodies, inhaled the god-awful odor then analyzed the two African American corpses with the eyes of a twenty-one-year veteran of Monroe's Public Safety Department. The male and female victim he determined had been deceased anywhere from three to five days---their bodies bloated and displaying acidic fluid leakage. On the male's body the larvae of dipteran flies wriggled in the drying leakage that had escaped his right ear and ruptured abdomen---blowflies and maggots were always the first to find the deceased when they were located outdoors.

The female's body although slightly bruised and heavily bloated in areas was charred in the vaginal area and on the hands. Her pink terry-cloth shorts were filthy and strewn further into the wooded area. It was apparent that she had been raped then murdered, the burnt hands indicated a possible struggle and the transfer of DNA. As did the incineration of her vagina.

Detective Gloria Duncan---Berman's usual homicide investigation partner patted her weave frantically with her left hand as she held a pen and tiny stenographic notepad in the other. Her teal Calvin Klein pantsuit and pink blouse were way too hot for the summer heat and way too expensive for an officer-of the -law---her Nine West heels were sensible and suitable. It was no secret that the thirty-six-year-old, curvaceous detective had a rich, sugar daddy and her job was a tool of leisure that sometimes caused strife.

Berman continued kneeling, fixated on a colony of ants that seemed to move from the male's body to their earthen community---back and forth. There were no detours or trails leading to any blood splatter because there was none---the detective knew that for the deceased male this had not been his place of expiration. And that before he had died, he had received a crucial beating. It was evident from the bruises and lacerations he had sustained about the face and head. But why? Who? More importantly, who were his John and Jane Doe---and why had their bodies been left just off the path that pedestrians took to and from the grocery store on the infamous Southside?

"Hey---Jim!" Det. Duncan shouted to get her partner's undivided attention. Berman looked up and shielded his eyes to block harmful ultraviolet rays. Duncan's eyes were concealed by a pair of gold-frame YSL sunglasses. "So far it appears that the male victim was shot four times---and the female twice. And she's wearing a Cartier ankle bracelet and fifty-dollar pedicure."

A young CSI that resembled actor Brian Austin Green hurried up the beaten knoll brandishing a small glass jar in a plastic evidence bag. "I found a jar that smells of gasoline---

"It's kerosene---not gasoline," Detective Berman interrupted. The young crime scene investigator looked ashamed. "This nose has been doing this for years. Still, you did good work---get that over to latent, have them check it for prints."

The CSI happily trotted off. Det. Duncan shook her head, her face bearing a smirk.

"Okay, you guys tag 'em and bag 'em---get these bodies to the medical examiner's," Berman stood as he began spouting orders. His muscular, six-four frame domineering---investigators moved hastily. "We already know the cause of death; we now need to i.d. these two. Check and see if any missing person reports have been filed---this young woman and young man were somebody's son and daughter---possibly someone's brother and sister. The girl was killed here---so somebody had to hear screams or shouts a few days or nights ago."

Detective Berman and Detective Duncan made their way back to his department-issued vehicle---a forest green Chevy Camaro that was parked in the cul-de-sac that was Summit Street. Inside the vehicle both detectives went into their investigative rituals---Jim popping his knuckles and rotating his head on his shoulders. Gloria reached for a bag of hot sauce-soaked pork rinds she had left on the dashboard to sunbake---she dug one from the bag, placed it in her mouth and sucked on it. There were about to be days of minimal sleep and minimal meals.

Berman exhaled before he spoke, his tart breath caught Duncan off guard. "You ready partner?"

"No---but somebody has got to do it," she answered with a mouthful of pork pieces.

"Well at least we don't have to knock on doors---most of the neighborhood is out here," Det. Berman said as he pointed to a group of elderly people standing about fifty yards up from where they were parked. He put the car into gear, hit the gas pedal and brought the car to a screeching halt in front of the rest home gang.

"How's everybody doing?" Berman asked. "Everybody good?" Det. Duncan asked with a polite smile, looking around her partner's head at the gray-haired, aged-face citizens.

"Well, police or not you need to slow your asses down---drivin' like a bat out of hell through here," a silver-headed elderly woman with distinct Native America features spoke up---she was tall and regal. She pushed up her glasses and leaned on the detective's car. "Who got *killt?* We tryna find out.

"Ms. Ruby, that's why we stopped to talk to you fine, upstanding citizens," Berman smiled at them all. "We have no idea who they are---we've got an African-American male and female."

"We know that much. We heard it on the scanner," a hunchback gentleman explained as he held himself up with a cane. Detective Berman could not take his eyes off the gentleman's t-shirt---which was emblazoned with "R.I.P. Pimp C" and an image of the southern rap legend.

"Well let me ask you to this---have any of you heard any gunshots, possibly a few nights ago, heard any screams? Are all your neighbors accounted for?" Berman quizzed.

"The girl's body is somewhat bloated, so many days having elapsed since her death---excuse my being too descriptive. But it's obvious that even with the body in the condition that we found it in that the girl was pretty, got her toenails done and wore expensive things," Det. Duncan added.

"You say her toes was done? The gentleman in the *Pimp C* t-shirt asked with a deep furrow in his mahogany forehead.

"Yessir---does that mean anything to you? What's your name, sir?" Berman tried not to show that he was ecstatic.

"My name's John Jason Witherspoon Senior," he stated as he straightened his back as best he could and poked his sagging chest out. "I served in the war, back in…

"John Senior! Hush all dhat and just tell the man what you know about dis young gal's toes---I wanna hear dis myself." Quizzed a bosom-heavy elderly lady whose granddaughter or grandniece had tried earnestly to give her Beyonce's caramelized hair-color. The finished product was orangish. No doubt she was the elderly gentleman's wife.

"Naw, I was just sayin' that that girl that live 'round the corner at the top of Green Street---I *seent* her toes a few times and they always done. She stay *wit'* that boy that sell that *shit*," he said vehemently.

"And what *shit* is that sir?" Detective Duncan asked as mannered as possible.

"Hol' up! How many times is few John Senior?! You said you *seent dhat gal's* toes a few times---how many?!"

"Awwwh-now, Joe Anne! I *seent* 'em one or two times," he pleaded. "I don't be *lookin'* at that girl like that---I told you."

"Two is a couple---you said a few, you lyin' ass heathen!" Joe Anne blurted as her massive breasts heaved and her orange hair bounced.

"Sir. Ma'am---please?! What does the guy sell sir?" Detective Berman persisted.

"You know---that shit! Crack-rocka Co-cola! But I ain't seent him or the girl in a couple of days---but that don't mean nothing, 'cause they always leaving to go get that mess. Stay gone three or four days. I watch Drug Inc.---they must be going to Colombia or Mexico to get it---that's where it come from. Not Africa."

"I don't believe they were travelling to Colombia or Mexico, sir." Berman interjected.

"Where else they gonna get it?!  I watch Drug Inc.? I know what the man on the news said," John Sr. said with anger in his voice.

"How do you know that this couple deals in drugs?" Duncan asked, watching as the elderly gentleman rested both hands on his cane and gave her a disgusted look.

"'Cause, lady---Bradshaw got a Cadillac and Volvo sitting in his yard, and he own a construction company. Perry got a late model Jaguar---he rent houses. That boy got a new Mercedes, ragtop—he ain't got no damn job! So, you tell me what he doing? Plus, people 'round here talk. He sell that *shit!*"

"Where does this couple live on Green Street?" Berman asked.

"Uh, top of the hill---apartment three-oh-four," the fair-skinned woman answered.

"What are their names?" Duncan asked.

"We don't know their names; they only been livin' here about two months---besides we try to mind our *bisness*."

The detectives chuckled at the latter statement and with their newfound information they thanked the community elders then drove away.

When they arrived at the cinder block, single-level apartment building. Detective James Berman felt the hairs on the back of his neck stand up before they were even out of the car.

"What up, Jim?" Gloria, his partner asked.

"I've got a feeling that this is where our guy was killed," he said somberly as he closed the car door behind him and walked to the door of apartment 304. Duncan close by his side.

Detective Duncan wasted no time knocking on the door swung open and a slender, mocha-skinned hooligan in a navy-blue Dickie uniform withstood in dreadlocks and an eye-patch stood in it. "Yeah, what's up?" He asked, almost irritated. The detective was instantly assaulted by the offensive odor of alcohol and high-grade marijuana and the sounds of Curren$y.

"I'm Detective Duncan with Monroe Public Safety Department---what can you tell me about your neighbors?"

"I can't tell you shit! Dueces!" He exclaimed as he attempted to slam the door—Duncan impeded his action with a stiff-arm. "Ay! Ay! *You on't* be *holdin'* no doors open *'round* here!"

"Little boy, I don't have time to be playing with you," she said snatching him out of the apartment with one hand and slamming him against the door frame where she held him. "You look like your ass is on probation as it is--- I smell the weed! And since you're outside the apartment and I smell the alcohol, I can now get you for public drunkenness."

"You snatched e outta my crib!" He pleaded, but Detective Duncan had no sympathy---she slapped him hard.

"Shut up! Now I'm going to ask you again--- what can you tell me about your neighbors?" Detective Duncan was forceful and fearless. The hooligan was almost on the verge of tears but when he saw his cousin now standing in the doorway his demeanor again changed.

"Fuck you---I can tell you dhat! You loose-neck *beeeeitch!*"

Street credibility was everything in the hood, but Detective Gloria Duncan knew that the young wanna-be thug's street credibility was store-bought and a few stories about being someone's penitentiary bitch---prospectively, would bring him back to his senses.

She spun him around, had him in handcuffs and was leading him towards the unmarked vehicle before he could think to scream *"call my momma!"*

"Where you takin' my cousin?!" The hooligan in the doorway yelled.

"To jail! The same place I'm going to take your ass if you don't get in the house and close the door!" Duncan announced---and he complied quickly, peeping out through the window blinds.

"Jim! We've gotta go! We've got our murder suspect," she smiled as she placed the one-eyed hooligan in the backseat.

Detective Berman got no answer at 304 Green Street, so he stepped lively back to the Camaro---with homicides time was of the essence. People became reluctant to talk and cases went cold.

. . . . . . . . . . . . . . . . . . . . . . . . . . . . . . . . . . . . . . . . . . . . . . . . . . . . . . . . . . . . . . . . . . . . . . .

The young miscreant, who Detectives Duncan and Berman had come to identify as nineteen-year-old, Lavon Little---*a.k.a.*, Lil' Roach, thanks to the photographic memory of an officer assigned to the department's gang unit. He had been sitting in an interrogation room for over an hour.

"You ready to go talk to the little liar?" Duncan asked as she placed her sunglasses atop her head. Berman nodded as he devoured an ice cream sandwich. Without a word he grabbed another from the tiny compartment within the mini-fridge and he and his partner walked into the purposely warm interrogation room. He tossed the ice cream sandwich to Lavon and sat down in the chair directly in front of him.

Both detectives waited quietly as the handicapped hooligan fidgeted with the wrapper on the ice cream sandwich. His first bite was rushed but he held the creamy cold morsel in his mouth in an attempt to bring down his elevated body temperature. He was hot.

"'Preciate the ice cream." Lavon said trying to sound *hard*.

"No problem---anything I can do to make you comfortable," Det. Berman said. His words saturated with sarcasm.

"Can you let me bounce *up outta* here? *Dhat* would make me comfortable." Lil' Roach said matter-of-factly.

"Sure, you can leave buddy---just as soon as you tell us what we *wanna* know."

"*I 'on't* know nothin'," he said before focusing back on the ice cream sandwich. He had already given them a fictitious name---and had quickly been exposed.

"I think you do, honey. Now--- you can tell us what we need to know, go home, and eat all the ice cream you can stand," Detective Duncan said politely. "Or you can keep your mouth shut, go to prison and get traded around the prison yard for pints of ice cream."

Lil' Roach laughed and lifted up his eye-patch, revealing a disfigured and sunken eye socket. "You funny, lady---but you must don't know *who I'm is.*"

Duncan open a manilla file folder and began reading. "You're Lavon LaRico Little, you were in and out of foster care and group homes until you were eighteen. At thirteen you were arrested for shoplifting, then at fourteen you were arrested for sexual assault, and a crime against nature---for that you spent six months at Dobbs Youth Development Center in sex offender counseling."

"A'ight, a'ight---you tryna play me now," Lavon---Lil' Roach said defensively as he flipped the eye patch back down over the empty eye socket.

"Oh, and that eye---it says that you lost that while staying at the Nazareth Home. You tried to sexual assault some girl and she stabbed you in the eye with an ink pen," Detective Duncan said dryly. She was beginning to believe that Lavon Little may just very well be their suspect. "You're a sexual predator---now I'm trying to play you."

Detective Berman just smirked.

"Who' owns the apartment building?" Duncan asked.

"I *'on't* know!"

She gave the ruffian an evil eye that forced him to stammer. "I---I *'on't* know! My-my aunt rent from the man. She know all *dhat* shit--- I *live wit'* her."

"Where's your aunt at now?" Berman asked with a sternness in his tone.

"She at work." His eyes were pleading.

"Where does she work? And what's her name?" Det. Duncan asked--- their efforts to tag team the suspect were working well.

"She works at the Pizza Hut over in Newtown, her name Brenda Little--- can I get a paper towel?" The remains of his ice cream sandwich had melted in his hand. It was hot in the tiny room and the detectives had made it about a hundred degrees hotter.

Detective Berman stood with his cellphone in his hand and left the room-no doubt to call Lavon's aunt.

Detective Duncan handed him a handful of paper towels and even began assisting him with cleaning himself up.

"Lavon, it would be in your best interest to help us out. Do you hear me baby?" she asked as she held the hooligan's hands in her own. Lavon could not take his eye off her succulent lips---full lips. Then his gaze fell to the cleavage that spilled out of her blouse.
"Yes ma'am." He answered as he shamefully looked at the floor.

"What are the names of your neighbors---the guy and the girl?"

"Duke---*dhat's* what they call him. *I on't* know his real name. his girl, her name---um, Candice. Yeah, *dhat's* it. Yellow bone chick."

"When was the last time you saw either of them?"

"I ain't sure, but it's been some days ago," he answered shaking his head.

"Who were they with? Any guest at their place?"

"Na—nah. Not *dhat* I can *thaink* of."

Detective Duncan looked deep into his one good eye. "Lavon, baby---I need you to tell me the truth. Who was at that house?"

"I mean, what you mean? *I 'on't* consider myself no guest *'cause* I t wit' dem like dhat," he explained. But he could tell from the look on her face the detective was growing frustrated and angry---and he did not want her to be either. She was holding his hands, touching him---she cared for him, he knew that. "I mean, like I was over there Thursday—me and *dem*."

"Who else?" Duncan licked lips and waited.

"I mean---basically *dhat* was it. Do-Rag came through---you know, we put a *lil'* something in the air---watched some television, then I left."

"Do-Rag? Who is Do-Rag?"

"I 'on't know his real name, but they call him Do-Rag 'cause he always got on a du-rag. It always match his clothes. He got all color du-rags."

"What time was it when you left the apartment?"

"Oh, 'bout seven-thirty."

"In the morning?"

"Nah, night, but it was still light outside."

"Did Do-Rag leave when you left?"

"Nah."

"Did he leave before you or after?"

Lavon froze momentarily.

"Did he leave before or after you?" Duncan quizzed.

"After."

"So, when you left it was just Do-Rag, Duke, and Candice in the apartment?"

"Yeah, "Lil' Roach answered shaking his head.

"What did you all watch on TV?"

"Huh?" Confusion registering on his face.

"What did you all watch on TV?"


"Uh, First Forty-Eight."

"Are you serious? That's my favorite show," Duncan said smiling at him. Lavon smiled back at her. "So, I take it you watched it from being to end, because that's a good show---you can't just watch half of it."

He knew she was trying to trick him. *The First 48* was an hour-long program---he had told her he had left the apartment at 7:30 a.m.

"I did. I only watched half of it *'cause I* left at seven-thirty like I said.

"Where'd you watch it? Chicago?" Detective Duncan asked.

"Nah, at Duke's crib---he got dhat big ass plasma TV."

"So, then you left at nine-thirty, because First Forty-eight doesn't come on until nine o'clock on Thursday. What were you watching it on? Tubi or Netflix?"

"Tubi?" A blatant lie.

"Wrong network."

Lavon snatched his hands away from the seductive detective and dropped his head, his *locs* concealing his face---she had caught him in a lie. Abruptly Detective Berman returned and motioned for his partner to follow him. Out in the hallway he beamed.

"The landlord is going to meet us at the apartment with the keys---I heard everything. Good work. I've got the gang unit checking their sources on Do-Rag. Let's let the little roach sit in the box a little longer, by the time we get back latent, and forensics should have something for us."

"Sounds like a plan," Duncan said with a smile.

Detective Berman and his partner left the police department in route back to apartment 304.

When they arrived, they found a bug-eyed, middle-aged white man sitting in a battered grey pickup truck. He eagerly ran from his truck, keys in hand. "I figured *ya'll* wouldn't want me to go in, so I just sat out here in my truck," he explained as he handed Berman the keys.

"You did the right thing," he said as he exited the car and patted the landlord on the back. "We appreciate your assistance. Since we don't officially have a search warrant it would be best if you unlock the door and allow us in---but I'm going to have to ask you to stay outside."

"No problem," he said accepting the keys. He moved swiftly to the apartment, unlocked the door and stood back.

Detectives Berman and Duncan entered the domicile with their guns drawn---what they observed was far more than they expected. There was blood splatter all over the cream-colored leather sofa, wall and floor of the living room. There were multiple sets of footprints. The glass coffee table was now a canyon of broken glass. There was even a noticeable indention in the cinder block counter that separated the kitchen and living room—undoubtedly from the ricochet of a bullet. Along the main wall that separated the two units was a large portrait---a beautiful butter-beige, Candice with her arms around a semi-handsome Duke. Both clad in Polo and jewelry.

Detective Duncan got on her cellphone and requested a CSI team---she could not help but notice that there was no big screen Plasma as Lavon had spoken of, only the remaining wires, cables and a few PS4 games. She also phoned the captain and requested a warrant for apartment 302---the apartment where Lavon Little lived with his aunt.

Detective Berman was still looking for identification and he would find it in the bedroom---Duke's driver's license which revealed his real name was David McDonald and that he had been twenty-seven years young. The only thing that the detective had been able to find of Candice's was an expired student identification card issued from Barber-Scotia College---Candice Ramsey had only lived twenty-two years of life.

When Berman returned to the living room it was flooded with crime scene investigators who were taking photos, dusting for prints and collecting physical evidence. Detective Duncan was examining a tiny reactor kit---its liquid contents reading dark blue. "It was definitely drug motivated," she said displaying the reactor tub. "We got that warrant---you want to go check out the aunt's or do you want to let a couple of these guys handle it? We can go back and work on our suspect."

"Let's let these guys handle it, we'll go work on Lavon."

Just as the two detectives were entering the precinct both of their phones sung to life---both rushing to answer their phone to report the information to the other first. "Detective Duncan---go ahead, she blurted. "Berman here!" He barked.

"Is that right?" Gloria Duncan asked as she smiled at her partner and gave him the thumbs up gesture. "I appreciate that buddy," Berman nodded as if the person on the other end could see his head motion. "I'll sing at your daughter's wedding---what about dance?"

"Again, thank you." Detective Berman said with a chuckle before his demeanor became serious. "My guy in the gang unit just faxed me a profile of Do-Rag---they're looking for him now. Let's get to my desk."

"That's great! Now guess what our guys found at Lavon's aunt's?"

"What?!" Berman was enthused.

"That plasma television that Lavon was bragging that the victims had."

"You've got to be kidding?!" Berman exclaimed as he and Detective Duncan scurried to his desk. There the fax machine had just spit out a still ink-damp, black and white photo of the suspect---Do-Rag. Even in such a poor-quality photo the impression of a durag line was visible across his forehead.

"Oh, our guys also found some of the same prints in both apartments--- latent is running them through the system now as we speak," Duncan explained as she studied the photo carefully---the young man in the mugshot appeared to be no more than fourteen. Wiley eyes and a menacing grimace that hid the true pain of his day-to-day life. "What's Do-Rag's real name?"

"Deuteronomy Beautiful Wadsworth," Detective Berman said as he burst into laughter. His face turning beet red. "I don't mean to sound racially insensitive, but is it some sort of *black thing*?"

"Is what some sort of black thing, Jim?" She asked somewhat offended---rolling her eyes with disgust.

"This kid's name---Deuteronomy Beautiful Wadsworth?"

"Deuteronomy is biblical, that's all I can tell you," Her tone was dry. Berman quickly changed the subject realizing he had *went there---"there"* was the place his partner had always warned him not to go.

"Says here that Do-Rag is sixteen---has an extensive juvenile record, gang affiliation, and has  had four arrests as an adult since turning sixteen six months ago," Berman said scratching his head.

"Arrests for what?" Detective Duncan asked as she shook her head in disbelief---still staring at the young black boy's photo---his adorable features hidden behind a demonic *ice grill.*

"Possession with the intent to sell and deliver and possession of a firearm on school property---shooting into an occupied dwelling, common-law robbery and resisting arrest."

"This kid is a menace. He should've been in jail. Why was he on the streets?"

"My guess---either a lenient judge or a low bond. You know how the systems is." A cellphone chirped and Det. Berman immediately reached for his.

"It's mine," Duncan announced as she answered her phone. "Detective Duncan---okay. I'll stop by thee in a sec'. Thanks."

She ended the call then looked at her partner, giving him a gorgeous smile as she slid the cellphone back into the pocket of her suit-jacket. "Let's go back in there and talk to Lavon---latents got his prints,

Deuteronomy's and Candice Ramsey's, our victim. Apparently, she had sticky fingers---an old shoplifting arrest. Duke---David McDonald had no prior arrest, whatsoever. Nothing in SID on him. And Josh Wilson's prints---I believe that's Lavon's cousin, the one at the apartment," she explained. "We've got his out of there."

"We need to send someone to pick him up," Berman said urgently.

"He's not going anywhere," Duncan said matter-of-factly.

"We've got the plasma that you had stashed at your aunt's---the victim's television. We've got your prints, Do-Rag's and your cousin, Josh's prints---all in the victim's place and on the TV," Detective Duncan said dryly as she rolled her eyes and shook her neck. So, you can sit there and play tough if you want to, little boy, but your cousin is *gonna* go down with you!"

"I mean, I don't really know what happened! I left! I mean when I did go back---they was already dead," Lavon pleaded.

"You're lying!" Detective Duncan yelled, pointing her finger in his face.

Detective Berman's cellphone rang, and he quickly answered it, never taking his eyes off of their visually impaired suspect as he ended the call even quicker and spoke slowly, "They're bringing Do-Rag in now. Guess where they picked him up at?"

"Where?" Duncan asked. Her demeanor now calm.

"At the mall in Concord," Berman smiled and folded his arms across his chest. "In the Mercedes-Benz! With not one, but two! Two underage white girls! We've got their asses!"

In Lavon's young mind no words had ever been spoken slower and they continued to echo in his head. He felt fervid, faint almost.

. . . . . . . . . . . . . . . . . . . . . . . . . . . . . . . . . . . . . . . . . . . . . . . . . . . . . . . . . . . . . . . .

"Deuteronomy—Beautiful—Wadsworth," Berman said meticulously. "Also known as Do-Rag. We know all about you and we know everything that happened you wouldn't even have me up in here--- *you'da* took my black ass straight to jail," Do-Rag explained vehemently as he leaned back in the plastic chair and rubbed his hands across his durag-clad head. His gray and white durag complimenting the black Dickies that swallowed him, his wifebeater and gray Jordan CP3 Tribute sneakers.

Age aside, Deuteronomy had the appearance of a decent middle school point guard---smooth-faced, lanky about five-foot-seven. "I know what this is---dem other cowards you talked to mentioned me, but they really couldn't tell you shit. You *scared 'em* up and they said my name! *I'ma* tell *ya'll* what went down."

"Well tell us what went down, Deuteronomy?" Duncan said dryly as she folded her arms beneath her melon-size breasts. Her suit jacket now removed.

"Don't play *wit'* me big titties," he retorted.

Detective Duncan was taken aback by his brashness.

"What?!" He continued. "I don't give a fuck about you!"

Detective James Berman had never met a suspect like Deuteronomy Beautiful Wadsworth, but he was not surprised by the *fuck-the-world* attitude. Today's young black males had been brutalized, antagonized, ostracized and miseducated for far too long. Love was not displayed so it was not reciprocated---they were fueled by hate. Do-Rag was fueled by hate. A true product of his environment. The detective's white privilege allowed him to ignore the realities of the world until it resulted in a case coming across his desk.

"If you don't mind, would you tell us what happened?" Berman's tone was apologetic.

"*A'ight*--- this how it went. Me and uh, Lil' Roach went over to Duke and his girl crib. We *was* over there getting smoked outw*it' dem*, we treated our noses a lil' bit---watched First Forty-Eight and was just *chillin'*. Duke was cutting up dope---talking *big boy shit*. His girl was *eyeing* me the whole time we over there. Anyway---he started talkin' 'bout how he got the dope game on smash, how *niggaz ain't seein'* the *kinda* money *he seein'*---the nigga ain't even from North Carolina! He from DC, somewhere. *Clowin'* us like w lame---talkin' 'bout how he snatched the *baddest* bitch, got the hottest ride, money stay in pocket--- talkin' about how he gotta put us on and throw us work or else we won't eat. Like we *starvin','*" Deuteronomy snorted as his murderous eyes looked into Detective Duncan's eyes. "Duke was just talkin' too reckless, like I don't get it in. And I do---now he *cuttin'* up about three ounces of hard in front of me and Lil' Roach---but he *talkin'* like he *sittin'* on a bird, like it's there in the crib. So, I'm just listen to this shit--- I'm getting heated. 'Cause then he start talking 'bout my bitch so fine she can straight talk *ya'll out ya'll paper wit'* out *givin'* up the pussy. So, I blank!"

"You blank? What do you mean?" Duncan asked as her and went to her throat. She was frightened.

"I blanked---I pulled out my pistol and I tell 'em---nigga, you a *sucka! Yo'* girl been on me the whole time we been in this piece and if you keep *talkin'* like you a boss I'ma clap yo' ass!" Deuteronomy said, growing agitated as he told the story---his hands moving illustratively every few seconds. "So now he pissed---he hop up off the couch talking *'bout I ain't* built like that, how he'll send his goons at me. *Fuck!!* I'ma goblin! Then he *askin'* her if she *suckin'* my dick! Talking about *she slummin'* if she fuckin' wit' me. Then he throw a stack at me---like I'm his bitch or *somethin'*. So, I start *pistol whippin'* him like he my bitch---then I blasted his punk ass!!"

"And Candice? Did you rape and murder her? Detective Berman asked, his index finger resting against his pursed lips.

"*Naw,* not really," he answered with a youthful chuckle. See, she was wit' it---like I said, she had been on me all night. *Lookin'* at me, *lickin'* her lips and *bustin'* her legs open wit' dem lil' ass shorts on, but I shot her man up and I'm tryna fuck her while he *laying'* there *dyin'* slow. She started *freakin'* out and shit---so I *gun-butt* her, while she knocked out, I take the pussy. But not really! *'Cause* she was on me until I shot her man."

"So, what happened after that? Because you didn't kill her at the apartment," Duncan said softly. "And why'd you burn her body?"

"Bitch, you *goin' quit comin'* at me *wit' that bullshit! Ain't* nobody burn no *fuckin' body! Don't be tryna* add shit," Deuteronomy said coolly. Bouncing from anger to calm. Displaying more of his street persona--- Do-Rag. "I put her and *ol' boy* in car, drove to the spot, dumped 'em--- me and Candice did the damn *thang* one *mo'* time. She was awake this time, but still on that hysterical shit. *Scratchin'* and *tryna* push me off, *screamin'* and shit---but that shit ain't do nothin' but turn me on. Straight up. Finally, I tell her though---I'm like if you keep fighting I'ma kill you. Act like you want it. Throw it back---and that's what she did, and when I finished I shot her."

"So, who set her on fire?!" Duncan persisted.

"Bitch! Is you hard of hearin'?! I don't know shit about nobody bein' set on fire---I shot the bitch!"

Detective Duncan was almost convinced that Deuteronomy was telling the truth about not burning Candice's remains.

"Well tell us this---who helped you carry the bodies to and from the car? I know you didn't do it by yourself," Det. Berman said matter-of-factly.

"Yeah, I did." Do-Rag's face was emotionless. Expressionless. He had done what he had done, and he did not give a fuck---plain and simple.

"Aren't you the least bit remorseful?" Gloria Duncan was searching his eyes for the slightest hint of repentance.

"What you think?" Do-Rag asked as he folded his arms across his chest.

Detective Berman motioned for his partner and the two detectives left the interrogation room without a word. But in the hallway, it was a different story. "He's a heartless little bastard!" Berman added.

"Let's go talk to Lavon, again." Duncan said as she led the way to the interrogation room where Lavon Little sat in oppressive heat.

Detective Berman bombarde the hooligan with accusation as soon as they entered the tiny room. "You lied to me! And I gave you an ice cream sandwich you sick *son-of-a-bitch!* You had sex with a corpse! You lied to us! You had sex with that dead girl---then burned her body!" The detective yelled.

"Why'd you do it, Lavon?! Why'd you burn her body?! She was already dead," Duncan stated through clenched teeth.

Lavon looked from one detective to the other with fear and shame in his eyes---speechless.

"Listen here, Lil' Roach! If you don't start telling the truth I'm going to personally see to it that they put you in a cell with a real convict that's been in the joint twenty or thirty years! And I'm going to personally put money on his books just to make sure he fucks you daily!"

Lavon was face to face with the detective and he could no longer fight back the tears.

"Why'd you set Candice's body on fire after she was already dead? And what was Do-Rag's role in that?" Detective Duncan quizzed.

"You know---you know why," Lavon stammered as tears streamed down his cheeks. "You watch First Forty-Eight---I was getting' rid of any DNA."

'Then explain why you burned her hands, she was already dead, she couldn't put up a fight---she didn't put up a fight, so why'd you do it?"

"I didn't want Do-Rag to get in trouble---and I didn't want to get in trouble.  he told us about what went down in the woods when we was *goin'* through they apartment *lookin'* for the stash, so I went down there to see," Lavon explained as he wiped tears and rocked back and forth. "She didn't look dead---I mean, it was dark, but she didn't look dead---

her skin was still warm and her eyes had life, so I did it to er. I fucked her, then I set her on fire wit' the kerosene."

Detective Duncan had heard enough about Candice's body being desecrated--- she cleared her throat before she spoke. "So, what did you all take from the apartment?" She asked, changing the subject.

"Me and my cousin took the plasma TV---*dhat* was it. Do-Rag took the dope and the money---I think he got half a *bird* and six stacks. Duke wasn't *holdin'* like he said he was."

Detective Duncan looked at her partner---tiresome, victory in her eyes. They were about to bring their case to a close.

• • • • • • • • • • • • • • • • • • • • • • • • • • • • • • • • • • • • • • • • • • • • • • • • • • • • • • • • • • • • • • • • • • • • •

"I've got to ask you---now that this is all over with," Duncan said as she leaned against the counter of the magistrate booth within the Union County Jail. "Do you still not feel any remorse for taking that couples like life?"

Do-Rag sucked his teeth and shrugged his shoulders, showing no signs of discomfort from being confined by handcuffs. "Remorse?! You still on that shit?! Remorse for what?! I can't bring *'em* back---they dead and *stankin'!"*

Do-Rag balled up the pink and puke-green documents---the arrest warrants that listed the victims of the two counts of G.S. 14-17 and the two counts of G.S. 14-87, and the release order that read---**$$ NO BOND**---he balled them up tight and tossed them into the detective's face. "They dead *an' stankin'!* Another Forty-Eight!" He screamed with laughter as two deputies led him to the change-out room.

# <u>DIRTY DIRTY AS TOLD BY DAREON</u>

*"Yamiiiii!"* Corrine yelled at the top of her tiny lungs. "Yami! Come *'ere!"*

"What you in here *hollerin'* 'bout, *Lil' mama*?!" The lanky, tar-black hooligan exclaimed with slight agitation---his long, thick *locs* braided into rows as he swaggered into the open bathroom wearing nothing but a pair of striped Polo boxers, then leaned up against the door frame and covered his nose with a long slender hand. He looked down at the seated crier---as lovely as she could be sitting on a porcelain toilet defecating.

"I need some tissue," she said politely as possible, displaying the deep dimples in her honey roasted face. Her arms folded across her naked lap. "Could you get me some? It's in the hall closet---please, thank you, sir."

"You lucky you so damn cute or I'd let you sit *dhere wit' yo'* ass all shitty," Yami said flashing a gleaming orangish-gold grill. "Forget *dhat. I'mma* let you sit *dhere.*"

"I'mma remember that next time you want some of this *shitty* ass."

"I'm playin' girl---I'm playin'," he admitted in a jovial tone as he disappeared to get a roll of toilet paper. "I *cain't* have *dhat* big pretty *yella* ass shitty. Never know when I might want to bite *dhat* butt."

"You nasty," Corrine laughed.

Corrine Robinson was a twenty-two years old Clark-Atlanta student, Atlanta-native and now a former stripper---Yami had frequented the popular strip club where she had worked for five consecutive weekends, even to celebrate his 27th birthday, and after a week of romancing the beauty he had persuaded her to quit and allow him to move  into her modest apartment, but with all the romance she did not allow him to occupy her residence without being sure he had the proper finances. And finances were not an issue---Yami's illicit past had awarded him stacks upon stacks of cash.

"Here you go, lil' mama." Yami said, presenting his lover of two months with a roll of Charmin's before vanishing to the bedroom.

"Thank you, boo!" She cheered---her voice carried down the hall like sweet soul music.

"Ay! What up?!" Yami shouted at the cellphone that rested on the bed where he sat---sliding his slender legs into his Amiri jeans. He could hear Corrine flush the toilet.

"What up, *partna*." Came the speedy southern jargon through the speaker-phone feature.

"We still on to meet at the strip club? *Yo'* man *gon'* be *dhere*, right?"

"Most definitely."

"Dhat's what's up---I'm *gettin'* dressed now. *I'ma* run somewhere real quick, but I'll be dhere. First bottle on me, *fo' sho'*." Yami explained--- he could hear the shower now running in the apartment.

"Now you *talkin'* my language, bottle on you."

"*Fo' sho'*---I appreciate you *introducin'* me to *yo'* man. I'll holla." The ruffian pressed the **END** button and resumed getting dressed---Amiri socks, wife beater and a brilliantly colored, yet hideous green, blue, mustard and powder blue Marni logo-knit tee. He walked over to Reliabilt 48-in. x 80-in. mirrored glass steel sliding door to the closet--- slid the door open and marveled at his medium-size collection of men's footwear. Corrine's shoe collection was abundant---all size 6 and a half. Then Yami selected a pair of Space Jam Jordans with yellow and tangerine accent, slipped them on. Awestruck---he moved to the mirrored door and began putting on his chunky diamond and gold chain and his diamond-encrusted Piaget watch.

Yami kept admiring himself in the mirror. Adjusting his chain. Fingering his watch. Pondering what it was he was missing. "Fo' sho'," he said to himself as he picked up a bottle of Dior Homme Intense cologne. He poured a bit into his hand---dabbed it on.

"*Ummmh*---you smell good, *zdaddy*." Corrine said abruptly as she wrapped her damp arms around his waist.

"Whoa! Lil' mama! You wet!" Yami announced as he broke from her grasp and turned to see what was going on.

"Save you some time," she said with a flirtatious innuendo. Her hands on her hips.

"Damn, lil' mama!" Was all Yami could say as he stared hungrily at her bald-shaven pussy. Her pussy lips looking swollen.

The Dade County-raised hustler was taken aback---the five-foot-two *miss* stood wide-legged and naked. Water droplets glistening on her honey-roasted, one hundred-forty pound, 34-25-43 structure---her perky C-cup breasts were eye-pleasing. Her body was flawless---not a bump, blemish, scar scrape or tattoo upon her young tender flesh. She was curvy, yet petite. Her face was past pretty and had awarded her runner-up to Miss Clark-Atlanta University---her Brazilian Curl weave which was shoulder-length looked long and natural.

"*Whatcha gon'* do?" She quizzed seductively. Biting into her bottom lip as she sauntered back towards him.

He exhaled loudly as he grabbed his hardening crotch. "I *gotta* go handle *somethin'* right fast first," he confessed with pleading eyes as she now stroked him through his jeans. He wanted to stay---dive knee-deep into her *wet-wet*, but he had to go out and get what kept her captivated---money! "Damn, I *'on't wanna* leave."

"I got you," Corrine said as she unfastened his jeans, unleashed his stiff manhood and leaned over to take it into her mouth before he could protest. First sucking him slow until she had his whole dick saturated with saliva, then she sped up---deep throated his manhood before spitting him out. "If I don't do it, you just *gonna* get one of them sluts in the club to do it."

She was correct in her prophesy and with that said she returned to sucking his dick---Yami looked down at her and smiled as the euphoric feeling seized is body and mind. He could not ask for a better *chick*---Corrine had a pretty face, a fat ass, a flat stomach, and she was about her business. She had book smarts and street smarts. It was amazing that such an angelic face could deliver such *hellacious head*---her jaws imploding and exploding with his dick.

Yami's story was like so many others---he had come from the bottom of the map. Had been living at the bottom of poverty for most of his life and had relied heavily on his innate survival tactics and his predatory skills had rewarded him with riches. All Yami's robbing and killing had finally paid off---and for the last thirteen months he had been living a new life in Atlanta, Georgia. His only illicit activity now---selling weight---quarter kilos, half keys, and whole kilograms. *Bricks.* His new life was good, so good he had even contemplated putting a baby in Corrine---if she would allow it. She was focused on obtaining her sociology degree and now providing her man with the best fellatio possible.

Yami wheeled his 1985 Buick Regal into the busy mall parking lot, the expensive system blasting---its gleaming exotic mix of tangerine and cranberry candy paint had been meticulously applied, emblazoning the classic car with tear-away ghost flags. He had the top-down exposing spectators to the cranberry-red ostrich leather bucket seats and visors--- the Buick was a sexy beast with its 400-small block Chevy engine and *Flowmaster* exhaust---a Sony seven-inch touch screen head unit, a Rockford Fosgate P400X4 Punch amplifier, six Kicker 12-inch Subwoofers, two 12-inch Eminence speakers, six 6.5-inch speakers strategically mounted throughout the ride and a 17-inch LCD monitor in the passenger door. But it was the paint job and the wheels that made the Regal standout, and above the competition---32-inch Yokohama tires hugged chrome rims.

Yami parked the Buick Regal in an available space and was immediately bombarded by a group of Atlanta misses with *g-fab* hairdos as he stepped from the car---true to southern body types they pressed their *super-thick* frames against the *stickup kid-turnt-hustler as* they made their way to their vehicle, giving him flirtatious glances as they did so. He gave them a nod---loving the eight-to one ratio of women to men.

He strolled into the huge mall and headed straight for the men's shoe store---inside the gamin quickly purchased two pairs of sneakers---#11 Retro Jordans and day-glow green #4 Jordans. Then he made his way to the food court where he was met by a sybaritic, full-lipped, cornbread-fed, Decatur-raised *yellow bone* who's hips, and ass forced the tap measure to register at forty-eight inches.

*"Heyyyy,* Yami!" She shrieked with excitement as she dropped her shopping   bags as he hugged her around her willowy waist.

"What's good, Kema?" He replied as he allowed his right hand to grip her plump derriere---she did not protest. Then he stepped back to fully take her in, she obliged the Miami hustler by pirouetting slowly in her red patent leather Sergio Rossi heels, tight white jeggings accessorized with a skinny red belt and a white artisan tee constructed of peek-a-boo sheer fabric revealing a passion red bra that seized 32DD breasts. Her wig was 100% human hair and *slayed*---a snow white, lengthy bob with red hearts emblazoned in zig-zag patterns. Kema was the truth.

"What you come in here to do? Buy me some shoes?" She asked, hands on her hips---already in possession of two Macy's bags.

"*Naaaaw*, I ain't *buyin'* you no shoes," he said sternly. Before displaying his golden grin. *"I'ma* buy you a bag---you like Coach, don't you?"

"Hell yeah! Stop *playin'*!" Kema exclaimed, pushing him in the chest playfully.

"You *wanna* get *dhat* Coach bag now? Or get something to eat first?"

"We can get *somethin'* to eat. I want some ice cream." She announced with childlike enthusiasm as she began leading the way to the soft-serve ice cream stand located in the food court---Yami followed behind her mesmerized as he watched her broad hips and juicy ass compel her frame to rock with raunchiness with each sultry stride she took. When Kema paused at the counter, her legs bowed backwards, and her butt cheeks relaxed and expanded invitingly---her stance was *mean*.

*Damn*, Yami thought to himself as he eyed her delectable ass.

"Yami---Yami!" She shouted to get his attention. Her grin seductive. "Will you stop *lookin'* at my ass and buy me a gourmet cup?!"

"Yeah. Yeah---be easy. I got you," he said snapping back into reality as he pulled a rubber band-wrapped stack of ten-dollar bills from his pocket and peeled three from the pile and handed them to the cashier.

"I want a caramel and vanilla gourmet cup gelato, heavy on the whip cream and cookie crunches," Kema told the cashier before looking back at Yami. "What you want?"

"Just give me, uh---give me, *uhhhh*---give *meeee…*"

"He'll have the same thing," she said dryly. Growing impatient with the Florida *dopeboy.* "You need to stop that Yami. It *ain't nothin'* but ice cream." She accepted the change for their purchase, their gourmet cups of ice cream, then she and Yami found a booth in the corner. It was the secluded booth that couples selected right before a Cheaters host would pop out from behind an artificial plant.

The two sat across from each other, eyeing each other flirtatiously--- Kema licked whip cream from her spoon slowly and seductively--- displaying a cookie-coated dollop of milky gelato on the tip of her lengthy tongue. Yami attempted to eat his creamy cold gelato but could not---the sexy *yellow bone* was *doing the most* with her own frozen treat. Swirling her tongue over the creamy mound of sweetened butterfat while she stared at him lustfully.

Kema ceased from devouring her gourmet ice cream interpretation. "So, what my girl *doin'?"* She asked, then went back to licking gelato from the spoon in her manicured hand.

"Oh, she at home." He answered coolly before taking in a spoonful of caramel and vanilla sweetness.

"That's my girl. My bestie---if she knew I was *fuckin'* her man she would have a fit." Kema said somberly before laughing. "This is some real *Maury* shit."

"What?! You *feelin'* guilty. You *wanna* stop?"

"No! *Noooo!* I'm just sayin'---look1 let's go get my bag *befo'* you start *trippin',"* she said dryly as she stood up and took him by the hand--- Yami tossed his cup in the nearby waste can and grabbed their shopping bags before Kema led him out of the food court and through the mall in search of a Coach handbag. She needed her *city girl* accolade for validation and justification.

Corrine sat in her well-furnished living room, watching the *Snapped!* marathon on the Oxygen channel---the scorn lover looked deranged on the 54-inch HD flatscreen mounted to the wall closest to the door. She was anxious for a commercial, so that she could utilize the home pregnancy test she clutched nervously in her hands.

*I don't know how he gonna act, but I'm finishing school. He might holler for me to get an abortion---and that's cool, too. But I'm finishing school,* she thought to herself as she listened to the narrator's fear-invoking voice as he explained the gruesome details. *Did she have to stab him seventeen times? Commercial!*

Corrine took of towards the bathroom---it was a complicated task, but she managed to urinate on the tiny stick. Now it was just a matter of waiting the instructed fifteen minutes. She finished up in the bathroom and went back into the living room---placing the home pregnancy test on the coffee table. The television program was now back on---and Corrine was finding it hard to watch. Her eyes kept darting to the white plastic device. It was like watching a pot of water, anticipating its boil.

"One line,'" she muttered, conspicuously peering at the test, wringing her hand nervously. "Let it stay right there. One line, that's it---just one line."

Her cellphone chirped abruptly. Her gaze intensified on the pregnancy test. She thought the test chirped, indicating that she was pregnant---she was disoriented.

Corrine pressed the speaker button and held the phone daintily a few inches from her mouth. "What's up, babe?"

"What's *happenin'* Lil' mama?" Yami's voice echoed through the cellphone indicating he was in a small room.

"Nothing. Just *sittin'* here watching Snapped, thinking about you."

"Hold up! You *watchin'* Snapped and *thainkin' 'bout* me---*dhat ain't* good." He laughed.

"You stupid," Corine blurted with laughter. "You know what I mean--- you so silly."

"Ay, look---I stopped by the mall. I was *thainkin'* about you and got you *somethin'*." Yami was somewhat lying, he had stopped by the mall. He had even purchased her a gift---but it had been Kema who had picked out the gift. "I'm *'bout* to go handle *dhat* other *thang* now."

"Awwwh, my ma so sweet," she purred. "I should go out and get you…"

Silence.

"Lil' mama! You still *dhere*?!" More silence. Yami grew desperate. "Lil' mama?!"

"Uh. Huh!"

"You *a'ight*? You was *talkin' 'bout* how you should go out *an'* get me, and then you just went dead." Yami explained with sincere concern.

Corrine stared at the two blue lines on the home pregnancy test as if she had tunnel vision---it was all she could see. *I'm pregnant. What am I going to do?* She thought to herself as she continued staring at the test.

"Lil' mama?! Corrine?! You *a'ight*?! Say *somethin'*!"

"Oh, uh. My fault, babe---this is a really good episode," she announced with a tinge of somberness in her voice. "I'm sorry."

"You *sho'* you *a'ight*?" Yami persisted. "I need to come home?"

"No, babe. I'm good. Make that money for mama." Corrine teased, trying to sound convincing.

"*A'ight* now. I'll be home in a bit. *Lul* you girl."

Corrine exhaled. She loved her man's deep south accent and how it sounded when he said, "I love you."

"I love you, too." She replied before ending the call and placing the cellphone on the coffee table next to the positive pregnancy test.

*When he gets home just tell him your pregnant. No! what if he wants me to have an abortion? My body, my choice,* she thought as she sat alone.

● ● ● ● ● ● ● ● ● ● ● ● ● ● ● ● ● ● ● ● ● ● ● ● ● ● ● ● ● ● ● ● ● ● ● ● ● ● ● ● ● ● ● ● ● ● ● ● ●

"*Lul* you girl," Kema mimicked with laughter. "*Awwh, ain't* that sweet?"

"Shut up. Turn o' ass around." Yami said forcefully as he stuffed his cellphone back in his pocket, grabbed Kema by the arm and spun the sybaritic *yellow bone* away from him, so that his eyes were locked on her ample ass---the secret lovers had conducted their trysts for the past three months, but never in a department store restroom---confined to a bathroom stall.

Kema unfastened her pants and Yami physically had to peel down her jeggings and black thong to expose her big, juicy yellow ass---he gripped it, fondle it, kneaded the huge orbs of flesh in his hands before dropping his jeans and boxers to his ankles and unleashing his long, stiff manhood. He pushed down on Kema's shoulders and she willing fully bent over, grabbing the toilet seat---the *miss* was wet between her thighs. But because she still had her jeggings on and could not gape her legs wide to allow Yami access, he had to thrust his raw hardness deep into her pussy. "*Ummmh—shhhht,*" Kema moaned as the hustler began stabbing his dick inside her---his long, slender fingers grasping the flesh of her haunches---thrusting. His lower back arched, his shoulder blades resting on the stall wall---watching the pornographic scene with arrogance as he delivered his dick to her hot wet hole. His dick sliding in and out of her womanhood at a rapid pace. Her pussy slurping and sucking loudly as he slammed his shaft into her, competing against her moans and rants. *"Oooowh—oooowh---awww, ummmh!"*

"Take dhis muthaphukkin' dick," Yami grumbled, pulling the pretty yellow rump to him as he continued slamming his manhood into her sopping wet pussy. *"Uhnnn. Shit. Pussy. Good. Shit!"*

There was a startling push to the stall door, someone trying to get in. the two lovers kept at it---Yami pushing forward and Kema throwing it back as he attempted desperately to *get a nut.* She looked back at the scoundrel, a salacious frown upon her face, a strand of hair stuck to her pouty lips as she was consumed by painful pleasure.

*BAM! BAM! BAM!*

"Is someone in there?" Came a voice from outside the stall.

Yami pounded Kema's pussy harder faster---forcing louder moans from his lover's mouth. His own groans growing louder as someone shook the door handle of the restroom stall. *"Pleasssse!* I can hear you! I have to pee!"

*BAM! BAM! BAM! BAM!*

*"Yammmmi!* I'm *comin'!"* Kema blurted as she rubbed her clitoris furiously. Yami's grunting and breathing were audible---stroking deeper, faster, harder---as if he was trying to knock the lining from Kema's pussy. He was almost there---about to climax.

"I'm going to get the security guard!"

Yami stopped mid-stroke and pulled out. "Come on. We *gotta* go," he said in a winded tone as he pulled his jeans up and slapped Kema across her ass. *"Dhis muthaphukka trippin'."*

Kema yanked and snatched at her jeggings until she had them back over her large derriere. The hustler exited the stall and Kema stumbled out behind him---both tried to compose themselves, grabbing up their shopping bags and synchronizing their evacuation. Yami opened the restroom door and the *cutty buddies* bolted past the elderly rail-thin black lady who had been protesting outside the bathroom stall.

"You should be ashamed of yourselves! Nasty! Heathens!" the elderly lady shouted as Kema and Yami fled.

In the parking lot Yami and Kema parted with a hug and went to their cars, which were only about thirty yards apart. "*I'ma* go by and see Corrine," Kema said pulling up beside Yami in her black Mercedes-Benz S600.

"Yeah, do *dhat*. Just don't be there when I get *dhere*," he said sternly. "I'll holla."

When Yami arrived at the Stroker's Club it was a little after 9 p.m.---warm and dusk out. But in Atlanta the strip clubs were where business meetings, business luncheons and dinners were conducted. Even birthday parties and bar mitzvahs were held in Atlanta strip clubs.

He walked into Stroker's---his collar popped, diamond chain and watch glistening majestically under the sensual glow of the club lights---the mixed aroma of cigarette smoke, liquor, sweat, burning cannabis and perfume consumed his nasal passages as 2 Chainz "Trap Check" blaring throughout the club. He paid the cover charge and swaggered further into the dimly lit center of carnal desire. Shapely *misses* gave lap dances to patrons and p-popped on side stages and sofas---

While others sauntered from table to table in florescent floss, G-strings, boy shorts, themed costumes and six-inch stilettoes and wedges. There was ass in abundance—shaking, quaking, bouncing, popping, and dropping.

"Hey Yami!" A svelte chocolate miss with a tooty-booty shouted over the music as she shook her derriere before a table of college-age guys. Yami was regular and known by practically every dancer in the club.

He nodded in her direction and was about to step to the bar when a pretty-face, doe-eyed *redbone* with what was probably the most devilish walk that any man had ever seen, and the ass of a Clydesdale approached him from the left---grabbed him gently around the neck and pulled his head to her lips. "DP and some dude *waitin'* on you at the back booth *ova dhere*," she informed him in her sweet sticky southern drawl---pointing to his right---his eyes followed her manicured finger. "I *ain't* never *seent dhat otha* dude, but something about him *ain't* right."

"He cool, Horse." Yami explained---appreciating her concern. "It's *bidness*."

"You sure? I just get a bad *feelin' 'bout* him. You good?"

Horse looked into his eyes for assurance. The deejay was now playing Big Krit's "Money on the Floor".

"He cool. I'm good---but you can put somebody on him. Now, I'd be better if you'd do that thang I like," he confessed with a smile. Peeling two ten-dollar bills from his stack of cash and holding them in front of her face. Horse, who's stage name was befitting due to her ass, stood five-foot-five, one-hundred and sixty-two pounds with measurements of 36-28-51. She stood in front of Yami with her backside to him, back arched, ass poked out and made it clap---made each cheek jiggle like jelly individually, together---then she let all the jelly settle at the bottom of her bottom.

*De-li-cious,* was all Yami could think as he looked at her ass lustfully as she clawed the bills from his hand. He then made his way to the booth, nodding to patrons that acknowledged him or

"Ay! What's good my nig'?!" Yami yelled as DP stood and he gave him a *dap-hug.*

"You!" DP stated flatteringly as he sat back down and pointed to his husky cohort who was still seated. *"Dhis* my man I was *tellin'* you about---Texas Petey."

"Texas Petey? What up, Texas Petey?!" Yami said with a hospitable smile, his gold grin glinting with the colors of the club's lights---he extended his hand. Waited for it to be accepted. Waited.

"I'm fuckin' with you, mane." Texas Petey confessed a slow scratchy southern drawl---chuckling as he accepted Yami's hand---his smile was platinum and VVS diamond encrusted, top and bottom. A mouthful of street success. *"I'm fuckin' wit'* you! *What's goin'* on, mane? Come on---sit down, mane. Whatcha  drankin'?"

"Good one. I was *thainkin'* you *ain't wanna* do *bidness wit'* a *nigga*---or *somethin'."* Yami laughed and took a seat next to Texas Petey.

Texas Petey, or Petey Jones, which is what a lot of people from his Southside neighborhood in Houston, Texas still called him---was thirty years young and forty years wise. A straight *get-it-by-any-means* hardliner. He was somewhat of a street general and had put in so much work in the streets that if he had wanted to, he could have been honored as a general emeritus ten years ago. But his physique did not necessarily represent that---he was burly and asthmatic with a large head---he was brown-skin with a neatly trimmed full beard.

"Not *wanna* do *bizness*? Not *wanna do bizness wit'* you?" Petey blurted, appearing offend. He adjusted the Houston Astros fitted cap on his head. "I'm 'bout my 'fetti, mane. Trust an' believe dhat, mane. What you drank, mane?!"

"Naw! Bottles on me," Yami announced as he slapped himself in the chest twice. Then raised his hand to summon a waitress---one swiftly arrived. "Ay, three bottles of Ace."

"Champagne?! We *'bout* to celebrate *dhis* money we *gon'* make. *Knowwhat* I'm *talkin' 'bout?!*" DP said in his exited speedy Candance as he nudged Texas Petey.

DP was short for Demontae Parker---the young freckled-face hustler was barely twenty-one and the owner of a black-on-black Bentley Continental Super sport convertible, which he had acquired by trading in a Lamborghini Aventador. The Westside Atlanta native like so many dope boys were now following the trend of driving foreign automobiles---a trend set by the infamous drug kingpin Meech. He had come up in the Bowen Homes Housing Project in Bankhead and at fifteen had taken *four-and-a baby* and hustled his way into a 1964 Carolina blue hardtop Coupe Deville---by age seventeen he had the Cadillac and his first imported vehicle, a cocaine white Mercedes-Benz CLK 63 AMG with a 6.2-liter V8 DOHC, 32-valve engine---a seven-speed automatic sitting on 20-inch Pirelli tires. Even though DP had the Bentley and the celebrity of a Shawty Lo, another Bowen Home boss--- DP's hustle had not progressed. He hustled only to live the life, balled like a ball player. His whole empire probably consisted of two kilos of cocaine and forty thousand dollars of ready cash, but he was DP. Young, fly and flashy. If the *Feds* swooped in, he would become Demontae Parker---inmate number yadda, yadda, yadda---old, dull and defeated.

The waitress returned with the champagne and Yami studied her for the first time---short and thick, not quite five feet. A new acquisition to Stroker's. she was not a female of Horse's dimensions, but still worthy of tips and attention, nonetheless. She was chocolate-dipped with aslant eyes, a fuchsia faux-hawk, twenty-one-inch waist and forty-inch hips in a neon spandex catsuit that made her massive *camel toe* appetizing. She placed a bottle before each hustler and began to make her exit. "What's *yo'* name, *lil'* mama?" Yami asked holding her by the wrist.

"Juice Box," she answered with her stage name as she shifted her weight to her left leg---her fleshy thigh bulged before the Dade County-raised dope boy's eyes. "What's *yo'* name?"

"Yami," he said smoothly---giving her a shiny smile.

"What *kinda* name is Yami?" She reciprocated the smile.

"Yami---it's short for Miami." His southern accent made pronunciation plausible.

"You from Miami?"

"*Uhn-unn*," he shook his head. "I'm from New *Yawk*."

"For real?! Nigga you *lyin'*!" Juice Box replied with bewilderment--- eyes wid.

"*Naw*," Yami laughed. "I'm *fuckin' wit'* you. I'm from Miami---Pork n' Bean Projects, Dade County."

"You need to stop," she giggled as she swatted at him with an empty serving tray in her hand. "You wrong for that."

"Why *dhey* call you Juice Box?"

"'Cause my *box* is juicy and wet." She giggled as the hustler's brow raised as he gathered a mental picture.

Yami released her hand and went into his pocket and pulled out a stack of crisp fifties wrapped in rubber bands. "Here," he said handing her seven fifty-dollar bills. "Keep the change, just make sho' you come back an' make sure we straight."

"Okay, thank you."

She sashayed away with sheer sultriness.

"Ay, Yami---you hear 'bout Smooth?" DP asked in a somber tone, speaking loud enough to be heard over the music.

"*Naw!*"

"He got forty-eight years in the *Feds* for *dhat* heroin possession *an' traffickin'* charge he had."

"*Damn*! What he have?!"

"*Fo'* keys of *dhat* black tar."

"What's good *wit'* you *shawty?!*" DP yelled---his attention now diverted.

"*Who dat?*" Texas Petey asked with envious eyes.

"Dhat's my lil' nigga Dareon." Yami interjected---speaking about the mocha-complected athletically built teen who had modelesque features--- almond-shaped eyes, high cheek bones and slight gap between his top front incisors. He was flanked by strippers---the jock waved wildly.

"Yeah, *dhat lil' nigga 'bout* to go to college, play football. He gone be a straight fool *wit'* it. He wrestles an' play ball out at Marietta High--- throw it, he go get it and come down wit' all ten toes in bounds."

Yami waved the star wide receiver over t the table---the youth moved towards them with athletic confidence.

"Ay, what's up, Yami? DP? What's up man? Sorry, I don't know your name," he said with polite urban dialect.

"What's up *wit'* you? *Dhis* Texas Petey---he good people," Yami said nodding at the Houston hustler---then gestured to the young jock with his arms open. "What you *doin'* up in here?"

"Recruiter got me up in here," he smiled. "Trying to get me to commit."

"What school?" DP asked. "Nah. Don't tell me. I *wanna* be surprised--- but it's a Georgia school, *ain't* it?"

"They are recruiting me in a strip club, what you think?" Dareon smirked.

"Georgia school!" Yami and DP chimed in unison.

"Here! Get you a couple lap dances," DP insisted. Handing him a thick stack f ones and fives.

"Get *dhem* lap dances in the Champagne Room," Yami said handing Dareon a wad of tens. "Enjoy yourself---just make sure whatever college you go to I get some tickets on the fifty. *A'ight?*"

"*A'ight.* I got you, both of you." Dareon said as he eagerly accepted the cash.

"*An'* stay *outta* trouble---and out *dhem* streets," Yami lectured in a fatherly tone.

"I got you," the future college football star answered. Fidgeting as he stood before the dope boys---anxious to experience the Champagne Room. "You know that *ain't* even my scene. I'm focused on football."

"*Dhat's* what up! Go have you some fun, enjoy *yo'self!*" And with that said, Dareon disappeared in the indigo glow that led to the Champagne Room.

"*Ay*, Yami---you and my man talk. *I'ma* head to the Champagne Room so ya'll can talk bidness," DP said standing up and nudging his cohort. "I'll be back."

Yami nodded to the young hustler, watched as he pulled up his sagging Celine jeans, grabbed his bottle of Ace of Spades and moved into the blue hue before disappearing.

"Yeah, mane---like DP *mighta tol' ya* I'm *tryna* cop three of *dem thangs*," Texas Petey said, both hands on the table, moving unnecessarily as he spoke. "But I'm *hopin'* you can let me get *'em fo'* the low."

Yami smiled---reveling in the power he possessed as a supplier. "What you *hopin' dhat* low is?" he asked before taking a swig from the metallic gold bottle he clutched by the neck.

"'Bout eighteen-five," he announced in his scratchy southern drawl. In simple layman terms he was hoping to pay eighteen thousand-five hundred dollars per kilo of cocaine. Yami laughed lightly at suggestion.

"Boy you a fool! I cain't do *dhat*---but I can let you get *dhem fo'* twenty a piece. You *ain't gon'* find *'em* for lower than *dhat*---nowhere!"

"Let me get *'em* for nineteen-five and I promise to come back and cop six of dem thangs at twenty a piece in no *mo'* than fifteen days. Come on, mane. I'm *tryna* get back in the race," Texas Petey pleaded with the Miami native.

"I'm *puttin'* you in the race at twenty a piece. *Muthaphukkaz* is payin' twenty-two all over the south---*an'* Kobe up *norf*," Yami said matter-of-factly. He knew whether the Houston hustler paid nineteen thousand and five hundred or twenty thousand dollars, he would be back---Yami did not need promises.

"*A'ight*! Damn, mane!" Petey exclaimed with a smile as he shook his new supplier's hand. "DP *tol'* me you was *'bout yo' bizness*, but damn! We got a deal though---let's get it."

"Let's enjoy ourselves first."

. . . . . . . . . . . . . . . . . . . . . . . . . . . . . . . . . . . . . . . . . . . . . . . . . . . . . . . . . . . . . . . . . . . . . . . . . . . . .

DP sat on sofa in the Champagne Room pouring champagne on the backside of a *yellow bone* with a jet-black mane and platinum-blonde bang who had her hands on her knees, her back arched, her garter belt lined with one- and five-dollar bills and her plump ass gyrating wildly to Young Jeezy's "Supa Freak" ---two strippers sat next to him kissing each other in the mouth sensually. An act they had been paid handsomely to perform. He whispered to one who appeared of Black and Asian descent, and she got up and sauntered over to Dareon who was getting the type of lap dance that was only reserved for professional athletes from a big butt, big-lipped stripper with blondish-brown kinky twists---she was allowing him to touch her where he pleased.

The *Blasian* stripper whispered to the one that vulgarly occupied Dareon's lap and the big-lipped *miss* swiftly slithered onto the floor, spun around to face Dareon and began unbuckling his belt and unfastening his Celine jeans---the young athlete could only smile as a pile o kinky twists fell into his lap and the salacious beauty began eating him alive, sucking his not yet mature manhood in a gluttonous manner.

· · · · · · · · · · · · · · · · · · · · · · · · · · · · · · · · · · · · · · · · · · · · · · · · · · ·

The deejay set the tone with Waka Flocka's "Round of Applause" played throughout the club as Horse did as the rap-song instructed and made her gigantic reddish-brown ass clap just inches from Yami's tar-black face---her ass causing at light breeze. *Clap! Clap! Clap! Clap! Clap!* Yami was mesmerized---and when the doe-eyed stripper bent over, grabbed her ankles and began quaking her ass cheeks and experienced the vibrations---inhaling the sweet mustiness she had acquired from her sweet perfume mixing with the perspiration due to hours of exotic dancing.

Horse laughed with enjoyment as Yami displayed his vulgarity. She raised up, but kept her back arched, attempting to clap her cheeks on the dope boy's face. She knew what Yami was into---the two had sexed on a few occasions at the Westin Hotel. He liked to give and receive *golden showers* and fuck her hard in the ass, which she did not mind, because when Yami *tricked off* he spent big money. He was a sexual deviant with deep pockets.

Texas Petey sat watching the Miami hustler with deep interest and disbelief while Juice Box rocked back and forth on his hardened manhood which she had covered with a condom before placing back in his jeans---an old trick of the trade. "What? You want Horse?" Juice Box asked looking back over her shoulder as she continued oscillating her ass on his stiffness.

"*Naw*---you good, *lil' bopper*." He replied---and she was. She was terrific at simulating sex and manipulating men's genitals and their *pockets*. The hustler smacked the stripper hard on the thigh and forced another dollar into her garter.

Horse was now on the floor on her hands and knees shaking her ass salaciously as Yami made five-dollar bills rain over her derriere.

"Are you serious?!" Kema blurted as she gave her friend a counterfeit smile. "You pregnant?"

"Yes," Corrine answered as tears streamed down her cheeks---the two sat in the living room of Corrine's apartment---the home pregnancy test that bore two thin blue lines sat on the coffee table. "You see the test!"

"I see it," Kema responded dryly. Unbeknownst to her best friend a tinge of jealousy was building in her curvy frame. "You know the results---why's you still got it on the table?! You can throw it away now."

"No! *I'ma* show it to Yami when he get home." She wiped the tear from her face and tried to smile. Kema displayed another smile.

"So, are you going to get an abortion?

Her question was deliberate and subliminal.

"I---I don't know." Corrine's voice seemed distant as she stared blankly at her friend.

"You should." Kema's response was rapid and blatant as she stared tried to appear sympathetic.

"So, you think I should get an abortion?" Corrine asked with a nervous look on her face as she gnawed on her manicured nail.

"Yeah! You *ain't* ready for no baby. You still in school," Kema explained as if she was the caring, concerned friend with poor consoling skills. Then she stood, hiked her low-rise jeggings up on her broad hips, bouncing slightly to adjust them properly on her shapely structure. "Look, *Pud'*---I love you, but I *gotta* go. You *gon'* be alright?"

"Um-hmm." Corrine stood to see her friend out.

"Remember what I said---you still in school. I'll talk to you later," Kema said as she embraced her best friend, gave her a kiss on the cheek-

--then smoothed out her snow white and red heart- emblazoned lengthy bob before walking out the door.

..........................................................................

Yami, DP, and Texas Petey *half-staggered-half-swaggered* out of the strip club---it was a little after 10 p.m. They were met by two country-thick *misses*—their wardrobes did not reveal anything, but one's duffle bag and the other's designer weekend bag made it easy to assume that they were strippers, heading in to start their shift.

*"Dammmmn!"* DP exclaimed as he flexed on the dancers and ogled over their luscious asses. Texas Petey grabbed his crotch suggestively despite being drained.

"Yami!" One of the *misses* called out as she recognized the hustler---then she dropped down, spread her legs like an eagle spreading its wings and popped furiously before coming back up. "I do private parties, too. But you already know that," she said as she winked and smiled in his direction.

Yami laughed. "We *gon'do somethin'---trus'* me," he said as he pulled two twenty-dollar bills from his pocket and placed them into her hand. She caressed his long black slender fingers as the money exchanged hands.

"We gon' do something," she purred in a sultry southern drawl. Provocatively pursing her lips---purposely. Yami, despite being a sinner noticed the stripper strongly resembled the cuter sibling from the gospel group Mary Mary---it was not until now that it had come to him. "I'm serious."

*"Fo' sho'!"* He answered eagerly as he gave her a nod before he and his cohorts proceeded to the parking lot.

"So how we *gonna* do *dis*?" DP asked as they stood before a fleet of automobiles. "What? We take one car? You got it now? Or what?"

*"Naw,* we good we good---*er'body* take dhey own ride. Unless you *gon'* ride *wit' yo'* boy---just meet me in the parking lot of the rim shop

across from the Waffle House," Yami explained as he gave DP dap and a hug---then gave the Houston hustler a dap-handshake.

"*Dhat'll* work, *mane*." Texas Petey replied as he patted his new supplier on the back and moved to his vehicle---a recently waxed red candy painted 1991 Cadillac Brougham, polished gold-dipped fenders, and trimming, sitting on Vogue *tyres* with custom mustard and mayonnaise walls and gold-dipped *swangas*---the wire rims off a 1984 Cadillac. A trademark of Houston hustlers and hooligans.

Juice Box came running out of the club, catching Petey before he got into his car---she gave him a business card, then scurried back into the club.

DP swaggered to his shiny black Bentley Continental as Texas Petey slid his bulky frame behind the steering wheel of his Cadillac. Yami checked his tag and his taillights before he got into his car---he was the last one to get into his vehicle and he planned to be the last of the three to leave the parking lot, Yami looked over at DP, who was parked parallel to him---DP was watching Petey, who was parked directly across from him. The Miamian looked over at Texas Petey, who was conversating on his cellphone. DP started his engine, and it was like listening to a ferocious feline sneeze---then he drove out of the lot, nodding at Yami as he passed. Texas Petey still had not started his vehicle when Yami started his and he knew then he had a decision to make---if the Texas native attempted to follow him all deals were off.

"*A'ight* my *nig'*," Yami mumbled to himself as he put the key in the ignition of his Buick. "I feel like you *gon'* try *somethin'* stupid I'm *deadin' dhis* whole *fuckin' thang*."

Petey as if acting off of telepathy ended his call and started his car---his system blasting the sounds of Houston's own, Grit Boys as he sped out of the lot, going let. Yami turned up his stereo and let the lyrics of Mo Pain's "Meet Me in the Tunnel-Remix" resonated in his head---

Young Jeezy's verse was like holy scripture to any trapper, it was still motivation to a thug. Then the *jack boy-turned-dope boy* wheeled the Regal out of the parking lot at a snail's pace, making a right turn.

Yami had made it only two blocks away from Stroker's when he heard the honk of a car horn. It was a distinctive sound, an expensive car horn---the ruffian noticed DP's Bentley parked at the gas station, so he whipped the Buick into the lot, turned down his radio and lowered his window. "What's up my nig'?!" He asked as he recognized the distressed look on the young dope boy's face--- wondered if the hustler was having a drug dealer midlife crisis, which usually hit at age twenty.

"You see ole boy on his phone?" he asked nervously as he wiped a bead of sweat from his freckled face with his right hand. His left still on the steering wheel.

"Yeah. I *seen* him."

"That shit don't bother you?"

"Should it?! *Dhat's yo'* man, you *s'posed* to know him---you brought him to me," Yami said placing his hand on his chest for emphasis.

"*I'on't* know. I just feel *dhat* as soon as we leave out the club, he all on the phone, *dhat shit ain't* right," DP said, now tapping the steering wheel with his thumbs. Abruptly Yami's cellphone chirped.

"Hold up my nig', "he announced as he looked at the screen. It read "*KEV*", which meant it was Kema, but she rarely ever called his cellphone. "Yeah---what up lil' mama?"

"You need me to come over dhere---right now?!" Yami exclaimed as he shot a glance over at the young dope boy who watched his phone conversation intently. "What fo'? what's up?"

Yami scratched at his chin agitatedly. "You *trippin'*! What you on? What got you *talkin'* like *dis*?"

Yami shot DP another glance---his mouth wide open. Then he continued his conversation. "Okay, you went by to see Corrine *an'*---what?! *Nah!!* What?! Don't say *nothin'?!* So, you *thaink 'cause* she pregnant I'm *finna* get you pregnant?! *Ain't* no way!!"

"Who pregnant, bro?!" DP exclaimed as he leaned out the driver-side window trying to extinguish his curiosity. Yami gave him a look that could kill, forcing him back into his driver seat and left him peering over the hand that shielded his face.

"Kema, *I'on't wanna* do *dhis* shit right now! *I'on't wanna* hear it! You *talkin'* crazy! You *talkin'* crazy *an'* I'm *tryna* handle *somethin'*---you is!"

Yami ended the call, turned the cellphone off and tossed it onto the backseat. "*I'ma* meet you *dhere*," he said to DP with irritation as he turned up the sound system and sped out of the lot of the gas station.

• • • • • • • • • • • • • • • • • • • • • • • • • • • • • • • • • • • • • • • • • • • • • • • • • • • • • • • • • • • • • • • • • • • • •

*Pregnant?! You 'bout to be a poppa, nigga---damn!! You can't keep doin' dhis shit my nig'---cain't keep trappin'. You 'bout to be somebody daddy---then you got dhis dizzy ass bitch talkin' 'bout she wanna get pregnant,* Yami thought as he drove to the meeting spot---keeping the classic Buick at a moderate pace. Checking his rearview mirror every few seconds to make sure he was not being tailed.

Yami hunched over the steering wheel and drove---selecting trap music for his listening pleasure. He had the *work* on him. He was just killing time as to not appear obvious. If his new client was aware that he was riding around with the cocaine he might set him up---either to be seized by federal agents or *jackboys*. He had to stay focused---the dope game could cause you to lose your head at times. Or get it knocked off.

When the Dade County representer eased the Buick Regal into the parking lot of Randy's Rims & Tires he could hear the sounds of rapper Future that came from two opposing parked candy-painted automobiles in the lot of the Waffle House. He glanced over---noticed a few thick southern *misses* fluttering and flaunting bright-colored store-bought hair and asses that they had gotten from their mommas or had bought when they had purchased their designer jeans. He then turned off the lights as he piloted the car around to the back of the rim shop---there he found DP and Texas Petey beneath a solitary streetlight, leaving against DP's Bentley smoking a blunt.

Yami had the car parked and was approaching the smoke session in a matter of seconds---he immediately recognized the citrusy stench of the marijuana to be that of *Sour Diesel*. Texas Petey whose bulky frame was on DP's right passed the blunt to the Miamian---he took a huge toke, his head went back, drunken eyes gazing up at the stars as his thumb and index finger pinched the butt of the high-grade hemp-filled Backwoods cigar. He took another toke---filling his lungs with the intoxicating clouds of tetrahydrocannabinol and cannabinol. ***KA-BLAM! KA-BLAMMM!!***

The blunt fell to the asphalt---the ringing in Yami's ears would not stop as he watched in horror as DP collapsed on the hardened tar. Instantly Yami found sobriety---DP's lower jaw and nasal passages had been blown off by two .50 AE rounds from Petey's Desert Eagle Mark 19that had struck him in the face. Yami's eyes were met by the smoking barrel---his throat was extremely dry, making it hard for him to swallow, fear choking him. His arms raised on instinct.

"*Yo' mane* was *workin' wit' dem* people,' Texas Petey announced in his raspy southern drawl---his eyes emotionless. "Did you know *dhat?*"

Yami was silent, scared out of his mind.

"Say?! Say, *mane*?! Did you know your *mane* was working *wit'* dem peoples?!"

Yami's gaze fell upon young Demontae Parker, what of him remained---air gurgled and hissed as it passed through the blood in his windpipe. He was fighting a horrid fight to live. The pavement now displaying a glistening puddle of the young dope boy's lifeblood. *TWACK!* The butt of the mammoth handgun had come crashing into Yami's forehead, blood gushed from the gash---he stumbled backwards---his hands went to his wound.

"Say, *mane?!!* You know *yo' mane* was *workin' fo' dem* peoples?!"

"*Naw*, man---I *ain't* know," he responded groggily. Tears in his eyes. "I swear *t'God!* I *ain't* know!"

"I believe *ya,*" Petey snickered. "But don't *ack* like you *ain't* seen it *befo'*---come off *dat work, mane!*"

"I-I—I got a kid, my *nig'*. My girl *pregnaaaant!*" Yami was becoming hysterical.

"I *'on't* give a fuck! Nigga, if you don't want the *lil' muthaphukka* to be bastard you better come off *dat work!*"

Texas Petey had the Desert Eagle down by his and was about to bring it back up to Yami's head. "It's in the trunk my nig'! It's in the trunk!" Yami exclaimed as he extended the husky *jackboy* his car keys. Petey's eyes lit up as he snatched the keys---*KA-BLAM!* The wiry hustler's feet left the ground as the blast from the hand-cannon knocked him on his back---reducing the weight of his three-pound brain significantly.

Petey stepped over Yami's lanky, almost lifeless body and quickly ambled to the trunk of the Regal, unlocked it and fished around until he found three tightly wrapped squares of cocaine stuff into an old speaker box filled with coffee beans. He placed the speaker box under his arm slammed the trunk closed and moved to his Cadillac.

Yami lay on the cool pavement losing his life---his body fervid from fever. His skull boiling from the gunshot. He could hear the jack boy's car start, then his tires screamed as he sped out of the lot and up the street.

*Corrine about to have my baby---damn! I don't wanna leave like dhis,* Yami thought to himself before haunting images of Hot Shot and Ball flooded what was left of his mind and he lost consciousness.

. . . . . . . . . . . . . . . . . . . . . . . . . . . . . . . . . . . . . . . . . . . . . . . . . . . . . . . . . . . . . . . . . . . . . . . . . . . . . . . . . . . . . . . . . . . . . . . . . . . . . . . . . .

Corrine could not stop crying as a thick-mustached homicide detective sat close to her on the sofa, trying to console her. "Ms. Robinson---I'm going to need you to be strong and answer a few questions, so we can find out who this to your boyfriend did," Detective Ramsel Horne stated calmly.

"My fiancé---," she said as she looked through the detective. "He was my *fiancé.* Yami was going to marry me once he found out I was pregnant."

"So, you're pregnant, Ms. Robinson?" Detective Horne asked before looking at his partner Detective Melvin Flatts, who was still standing. Flatts, unlike his partner was clean-shaven with a bald head---he was trim and tall, six-eight. He stood like a ball player on a perpetual time-out. Both white men had pasty skin signifying that they avoided the hot Georgia sun by staying inside, doing paperwork, and sleeping during the day and hunting murder suspects at night. "Ms. Robinson---didn't you say you're pregnant?"

"Um-huh," she answered as she wiped her eyes and rocked nervously back and forth. Wrapped in her own arms tightly for comfort. "I'm *pr-pregnant*."

"We have an officer going to pick up a---Kema Jones and bring her down to the station for questioning. Do you know Kema Jones or why she'd be the last person to call your fiancé? Or why he would have her saved in his phone as Kev?"

Detectives were very insensitive when it came to solving a case.

Corrine's face went from lachrymose to anguished disbelief---she was befuddled. "Ms. Robinson?" Detective Horne persisted.

"Oh---uh, Kema is my best friend," Corrine answered as she sniffled and snorted. "But I don't know why her number would be in his phone."

"What can you tell us about Demontae Parker?" Detective Flatts asked. Placing his hands into the pockets of his brown slacks. He often felt that those being questioned found his hands intimidating and suppressed important details.

"Who?" Corrine looked cluelessly at the towering detective.

"Demontae Parker---street name DP." He said matter-of-factly.

"DP?! I know him. What about him?! He, did it?!" She quizzed in rapid fashion.

"No. No, ma'am---as we told you we're homicide detectives, and Demontae was with your fiancé ---but he didn't make it. Demontae had some criminal issues he was trying to resolve by cooperating with an agency..." Detective Flatts paused---as if trying to compose the right words.

Corrine still had a look that registered confusion.

"What my partner is saying, Ms. Robinson, is Demontae Parker was cooperating with the *Feds*---he was going to give up your fiancé." Detective Horne explained as he used his hands to illustrate his words. "Look---we know what your fiancé LaRoyal Daniels was doing. He was selling kilos of coke... cocaine. I'm guessing he and Demontae were partners---the kid's twenty-one with a Bentley and no source of income---but that doesn't change the fact that someone killed him and attempted to kill your fiancé. And I believe it was someone they were doing business with."

"Maybe Kema had something to do with it? Maybe she set them up?"
Detective Flatts added.

**************2 DAY LATER***********

"Kema---the police told me you *wasn't* involved in Yami's *shootin'*, but you still ain't never tell me why you *was* callin' Yami phone the night he was shot." Corrine said dryly as she and her best friend stood in the hallway of the intensive care unit. Kema stared at her friend's Jimmy Choo heels--- avoiding eye contact. "Answer me, Kema?!"

"I wanted a baby!" She blurted, gaining stare from an old couple and a pigeon-toed registered nurse."

"A baby?! What Yami *gotta* do *wit'* you *wantin'* a baby?! That don't make sense, Kema!"

"Kema?!" Corrine screamed in her face.

"Is there a problem, ma'am?" Asked a hulky black orderly who had stopped pushing a wheelchair-bound elderly lady to see what all the fuss was about.

"Yeah! *Damyyyyam!*" Kema announced vehemently with neck rolls and pouting lips.

"Fuck you! I'm from Decatur, *bitch!* Don't get it twisted!" The hospital orderly barked before strolling off with his chauffeured patient laughing hysterically.

"I know this nigga---" Kema exclaimed before being held back by Corrine.

"You need to tell me! What Yami *gotta* do with you *wantin'* a baby?!"

Kema nervously toyed with her nails, then cleared her throat. "When you told me you were pregnant---it made me want a b aby," she explained.

"Okay, and?! Where does Yami come in to all this?" Corrine asked, gesturing with her hand for her friend to continue.

Kema exhaled, shifted her weight. "Me and Yami been *fuckin'* around!"

Corrine's jaw dropped and her eyes bulged.

"Are you serious?! Bitch?! Are you serious?! Kema?! Are you serious?! Oh, God---are you *fuckin'* serious?"

Corrine collapsed right there in the hallway---crying uncontrollably. Kema knelt at her side to comfort her, placed her hand on her friend's shoulder.

"Don't touch me! You ratchet! Don't touch me---scandalous bitch! I can't believe you did me like that! You wrong! You wrong, Kema! You wrong! *Gwone!! Gwone* Kema!" She screamed, kicking and swinging her arms at Kema.

"I'm sorry, *Pud'*." Kema said softly---stood, hiked her silver liquid leggings up on fer hips and walked away from her friend quickly---her Jordan Retro # 3s squeaking loudly on the well waxed floor as she descended the hallway.

Corrine gathered herself from the floor and shuffled slowly into Yami's hospital room---she was immediately assaulted by the sterile stench of antiseptic and the constant nerve-racking beeping of the EKG machine as it monitored Yami's vital signs. She stood at the foot of his bed and tried to find a trace of the man she had once known---gone were the jewels and diamonds. There were tubes running into his arms, nose, and mouth. His *locs* no longer existed---those that were not lost because of being shot in the head, had been shaved off in preparation for the emergency surgery that had taken place. Yami's head was now bandaged and misshapen---the right frontal lube sunken where a portion of his skull had to be removed, as had the damaged portion of his brain. His weight had dropped drastically in two days---his once wiry frame was now sickly. He resembled a mummy.

Corrine wiped away more tears as she examined the man she loved, searching for the man she had been loving---questioning her love as she thought about his infidelity and the tragedy that had struck him. Did she want to be with this new man? This disabled man? Did she love this *now* shell of a man? Did she want to have a child by this man that was now child like himself?

* * *

"Who this?" Juice Box asked as she held the cellphone in front of her as she steered her Mercedes M-Class through traffic.

"Who *dis?!*" Slow. Southern and raspy.

"Jazmine---but you called my phone."

"Jazmine?! *Dis ain't* the *lil' bopper* From Stroker's---Juice Box?"

"It is. And I know who I'm *talkin'* to," she proclaimed cheerfully. "This Texas Petey."

"*Shol'* is. *Ay*---what you got me on speaker phone?" He asked in the raspy drawl that she remembered so well.

"Yeah---I'm *drivin'* on my way to work. It's not a problem, is it? *Ain't* nobody in the car but me."

"*Naw,* you good---you was just *soundin'* boxed-in an' had an echo."

"So, what's up?' Jazmine's tone was still vibrant.

"*Sheiiit---ain't nothin'.* I'm tryna fly you out."

"To where?!" She sounded ecstatic.

"*Outchea!* Houston, Texas, baby! Spend some time wit me. Let me spend some money on *ya'*." Texas Petey said with coarse confidence. "I'll fly you out."

"You back in Texas and you *wanna* fly me out?!" Juice Box aske in disbelief. The *odds*.

"Yeah." Petey replied.

"I'd rather take the bus. *I'ma* send my Cash App." *Jazmine* stated as she wheeled her luxury SUV into the parking lot of the strip club. "Wait! I don't know if I should---I don't know you like that. You know what I'm *sayin'*?"

"Yeah, I know what you mean, *lil' bopper*--- but damn! Don't do me like *dhat*. Didn't I spend dem *bands* on you when I was in the club?"

"Yeah," she responded in a childlike voice. "You did spend that *bread.*"

"So, what it do?! You gone come let me show you how we do it in H-Town? I'm *finna* Cash App you eight hunned right now!"

"I'm down, but it's going to be tomorrow. I'm at work now." Jazmine said as she pulled into the parking lot reserved for dancers.

"Okay---cool. See you *t'morrow.*" Petey said.

"That's what's up!" Jazmine replied as she grabbed her eco-friendly cotton canvas designer bag from the front passenger seat. Then she exited the M-Class and sauntered into the club.

• • • • • • • • • • • • • • • • • • • • • • • • • • • • • • • • • • • • • • • • • • • • • • • • • • • • • •

Corrine sat curled up in the lounger in Yami's hospital room, her knees up to her breasts and her arms wrapped around them tightly--- her eyes puffy and red from many tearful moments. She watched as nurses tended to Yami---pondering whether she could take on such a responsibility of a child.

"Excuse me," Corrine croaked. "Excuse me---could either of you refer me to an OB-GYN?"

"Sure, *sug'*. I can refer you to one," spoke the white nurse with the orangish salon tan and dirty blonde hair. "You need to see Doctor Thatcher downstairs on the second floor---I couldn't think of a *better-lookin'* man to show my treasure." She nudged the husky black nurse---both laughed.

"Treasure?!" The blacked nursed huffed. "Janice, you should call it your lost treasure, it's been a long time since any man has seen it."

The two women laughed harder before Janice became serious, recognizing the pain in Corrine's eyes. "Hush, Beulah! Sug', he's on the second floor. He won't be hard to find."

Corrine slowly left Yami's room, saying nothing to the nurses she made her way to the elevator---contemplating her life as she boarded the elevator---her destination the second floor.


The sorrowful *miss* stepped of the elevator and in minutes found the handsome obstetrician-gynecologist flocked by young female registered nurses and candy stripers. Corrine was unsure of his nationality. Polynesian and African American, maybe?

"Doctor Thatcher?!" Corrine called out---drawing the physician's attention and a look of disdain from the nurses and volunteers.

"Excuse me, ladies." He said with a polite smile as he moved towards the distressed-looking *miss*. Each nurse trying to brush up against the good doctor who always seemed to smell of apricots and bergamot.

"What can I do for you?" He asked as he ushered Corrine in the direction of his office with the clipboard he had in his hand.

"*Ummh*---I'm pregnant."

"Congratulations. That's wonderful. Right in here," Dr. Thatcher announced as he opened the door to his office and waited as she hesitantly crossed the threshold---watching her expression intently. "Miss?"

"Robinson---Corrine Robinson," she answered as she sat down in one of two chairs across from his desk.

"Ms. Robinson, you don't seem too enthuse about your pregnancy." He gave her a deciphering look. Then he leaned back so that he was sitting atop his desk---legs crossed, arms folded and his hands resting on his face, his index finger extended to his temple as if in deep thought.

"Ms. Robinson?"

"I don't---I'm not," Corrine answered matter-of-factly. "I mean, I was at one point---but my fiancé was shot and is ICU, almost brain dead. I don't want to raise a child by a man that's now a child himself."

"I love him…" Her words trailed off---tears welled in her eyes as she looked through the doctor. "I want an abortion."

"Do you understand what you're saying?" Doctor Thatcher inquired. His exotic features sympathetic, but Corrine did not notice.

"I want an abortion," she said dryly---her eyes now menacing, tear-leaking slits were focused on the doctor. She continued her protest. "I want an abortion! I want an abortion! I! Want! An abortion!"

Doctor Thatcher placed the clipboard on his desk, and slowly and cautious enveloped Corrine in his brawny arms as he knelt before her. "*Shhh. Shhh*. I understand," he cooed her as he rubbed her back. "Corrine---I understand."

Corrine had been on the verge of hyperventilating until the doctor's reassuring petting ceased it.

"Ms. Robinson, if you've thought this through and you're sure this is what you want to do, I'll perform the procedure. I'll just have to have you meet with one of my nurses, give her your insurance information and let her run some standard test, see how far along you are. How does that sound?"

"Can we do it today?" Corrine exclaimed.

Doctor Thatcher withdrew from the embrace---looked at the distraught *miss* with rational disbelief. She knew what she wanted to do yet she was torn. "I'm sorry, Corrine. The procedure can't be done today," he is replied---patting her on the back as he stood. "Let's get you to one of my nurses, maybe we can fit you in sometime tomorrow."

● ● ● ● ● ● ● ● ● ● ● ● ● ● ● ● ● ● ● ● ● ● ● ● ● ● ● ● ● ● ● ● ● ● ● ● ● ● ● ● ● ● ● ● ● ● ● ● ● ● ● ● ● ● ● ● ● ● ● ● ● ● ● ● ● ● ● ● ● ● ● ● ● ● ● ● ●

"I'm here," Juice Box---Jazmine announced into her recently purchased Trac Phone as she stepped off the Greyhound bus in Houston, Texas--- her finger jammed into her fiber optic-free ear. The bus station was bustling---people from all walks of life going and coming. Diesel engines grumbling, brakes hissing, people speaking in many tongues--- Spanish, Ebonics and Texas Twang. The area of 6590 Southwest Freeway smelled of dust and diesel fuel. "I'm *finna* call Petey now so he can pick me up---oh, I already know. Handle my business *an'* get back."

Jazmine ended her call and picked her backpack up off the pavement and slung it over her left shoulder---then she dialed Texas Petey. Stood there as the phone rang---her fuchsia hair styled in a faux French twist, which was a blazing one-hundred-and-ten-dollar French twist with a pompadour, highlighting her pretty chocolate face and aslant eyes. Her four-eleven succulent, thick frame fashioned in a sleek snow-white Moncler Grenoble down jacket, bright pink hip-hugging jeggings, and white and pink Moon Boot boots. She looked good, but she would have to change---Houston was not quite as cool as Atlanta was.

■ ·································································

"Hey---you!" Horse said enthusiastically as she could---swaggering into the hospital room looking stunning in faux fur-trimmed Coach Scout wedges, 7 for All Mankind denim jeans that her 51-inch hips and ass appeared to be poured into and a plum and cream leopard-print wool and mohair Balenciaga sweater. Her hair was flawless---twenty-four inches of Brazilian bundle. "I said, hey you!"

Yami as sickly and incompetent as he now was managed to slowly turn his head towards the large window---shame and insecurity were still able to register in what was left of his mind.

Horse approached the *jackboy-turnt-dopeboy's* bed brandishing a spurious smile---then the doe-eyed yellow bone leaned in and kissed the misshapen left portion of his head. Yami winced. "*Ooh*, you wrong for dhat! You act like I just finished *suckin'* a dick."

She giggled, trying to make of the somber situation---taking his hand into her own. The electrocardiograph keeping a steady and audible record of Yami's heartbeat. Then she spoke softly, yet confidently. "Yami, I'm *takin'* care of that situation you told me to handle, so don't you worry *'bout nothin'*."

·································································

Texas Petey wheeled the shiny red Cadillac Brougham into the parking space of the Ramada In and parked---he and Jazmine exited the automobile. Jazmine unfamiliar with the area moved more cautiously than husky hooligan in the Houston Astros cap--- conspicuously looking around.

"You good, *lil'* bopper." Petey said in his gravelly drawl, ambling to his hotel room as he brushed lint from his Amiri tee. "You in my city." His tone almost braggadocious.

He stopped in front of the beige door affixed with gold numbers that read "**222**" ---admired the succulent stripper lustfully before swiping the keycard and opening the door.

"Come on in, lil' bopper." He motioned for her to enter the hotel, stepping back so that back so that she had an unimpeded passageway. Jazmine with her backpack on her shoulder smiled seductively, then went into her Juice Box persona---her walk grew more titillating as she sauntered past Texas Petey and into the room. She looked around with surprise--- the room was spacious and elegant with two floral-quilted twin beds and walls painted in eye-catching earth tones. One of which held a sleek HD flat-screen that appeared to be no more than 32-inches---Juice Box eagerly pranced over to the bed where the remote sat, turned on the television and sat on the bed.

Texas Petey grinned, flashing his diamond and platinum grill as he closed the door and moved towards the salacious dancer---brandishing a small jar of high-grade marijuana. "*Dis dat* OG Kush," her lap and pulling a package he proudly proclaimed. Tossing the jar into her lap and pulling a package of mango-flavored blunt wraps from his pocket before popping down on the bed close to her. "Roll up."

He took the remote and turned to a television network that showed videos twenty-fours a day. Texas rappers, so as *chopped* and *screwed* melodies filled the room Juice Box broke up the buds, lined them along the blunt wrap, rolled it up and licked it to seal in the aromatic *Kush*.

Texas Petey leaned back on the bed and rubbed his pockets, attempting to locate a cigarette lighter. "Damn!" he blurted as he found none---then he stood, pulled the Astros snapback down slightly. "Ay! *I'ma* run *'cross* the street t the convenient *sto'*---get a lighter *an'* some rubbers."

With that said he disappeared out of the hotel room---too lazy to run or even walk, he drove fifty yards across the street to the store, made his purchases and quickly returned.


"What it do?! Got *dem* rubbers *an'* a lighter!" he announced as he stormed into the room waving a box of Magnum condoms in the air--- Juice Box lay across the bed, naked. "*Dayyeeem!*"

Her smooth chocolate skin radiant and tightly stretched over her young curvaceous frame---her aslant eyes gave her Asian characteristics and thy were orgasm-inducing. Her fuchsia hairdo was flamboyant and sexy. She giggled, then lifted her right leg towards the ceiling---her fuchsia-dyed, cropped pubic hair on display. Along with her plump hungry pussy.

"You *'on't* need a lighter---I'm already on *fiyah*," Juice Box teased as she pushed her index and middle finger into her wetness. Petey swallowed hard before working his face into a devious grin that gleamed brilliantly---he walked coolly over to the bed.

*All the bad bitches wanna give me head*, Petey thought to himself as he stood over her---not knowing whether it had come rom a rap-song or if he had made it up. By the time the FN Hi-Power 9mm semi-automatic handgun in Jazmine's hand registered in his head. ***POPT! POPT!*** It was too late. His obese body fell forward, forcing the sultry assassin to leap out of the way as Texas Petey collapsed on the bed---his top oozing a red liquid more vital than hot sauce.

Jazmine placed the pistol on the bed, walked over to the sink in the foyer that led to the bathroom---looked at herself in the mirror over the sink. There were droplets of blood on her face and breasts. She trotted to her backpack, grabbed a packet of wet wipes, then strutted hurriedly back to the mirror and began cleaning herself---tossing the used wipes into the lined waste basket. Jazmine sped to her backpack and quickly dressed in new attire---back to the waste can she went with the clothes she had arrived in---she tossed them in the trash. She then scanned the room, gathered up all her belongings, the trash bag from the waste basket and the 9mm, which she wrapped in a hand towel---wiping it furiously before tossing it in the tiny trash bags.

Jazmine slung the backpack onto her shoulder, looked around the hotel room once more---calculating and contemplating with the waste bag of her incriminating evidence in her hand---then walked out of the room inconspicuously, being sure to use the sleeve of her hoodie to open and close the door as she exited.

Jazmine had disposed of the trash bag of evidence---her clothing, the gun, and the prepaid cellphone. She had even drove the deceased's vehicle to a secluded area and torched it. Then she had taken a taxi to the bus station and was now on her way back to Atlanta, Georgia.

. . . . . . . . . . . . . . . . . . . . . . . . . . . . . . . . . . . . . . . . . . . . . . . . . . . . . . . . . . . . . . . . . . . . . . . . . . . . . . . . . . . . .

"Wake *yo'* ass up," Juice Box---or rather Jazmine said softly as she slapped Horse's leg. The sleeping stripper's eye fluttered open---then she focused on the pretty killer. 'Wake up! You hear me?! It's done."

"Good," Horse said groggily as she stretched in the reclined chaise before sitting up straight. She looked over at Yami, he was asleep---probably roaming through a collection of half thought and memories. Horse stood. "You handled everything as I explained?"

"Exactly." Jazmine answered. Trying to seem energized, but her eyes expressed her need for sleep. Horse gave her a much-needed hug and patted her on the back. Then they both looked at Yami sympathetically---their arms around each other.

"You, okay?" Horse asked softly.

"I'm good."

"Good. You did good---Yami good people. Texas Petey got what he deserved. You do dirt, you get dirt. Straight like *dhat*," Horse said matter-of-factly…

**THE END…OR IS IT?**

## About the Author

Silky Allen is an established author and writer who has had his work published in Ebony Magazine and Ozone Magazine. He is the founder and president of Struggle Street Publishing Company and has published several literary pieces under the Struggle Street flagship. His creativity has led to the publishing of his erotic E-series "Chasing Pavement", available on Kindle Vella, and the sensational paperback "WILD ASS BREE: A Bus Ride Read", available on Amazon.

Mr. Allen has attended South Piedmont Community College, Halifax Community College, the illustrious Winston-Salem Barber School and the innovative Forsyth Technical Community College---briefly studying graphic arts and imaging before a major change to radio broadcasting and production and a 4.0 GPA recognition award.

He has flown in helicopters over the Appalachian Mountains (Tennessee and North Carolina), tandem skydived in Salisbury, swam with the sharks infesting Myrtle Beaches shoreline, *catcalled* with the lions and tigers at the Animal Park at the Conservators Center, and rode several Saddlebred and Steeplechase courtesy of his courage, funds, and Legacy Saddle breeds.

He is a caring father to his son, Dareon, and an extraordinary uncle to his many nieces and nephews. Despite an eighteen-year stint in North Carolina's prison system he has persevered and prevailed. Came out to be successful in every aspect of life and every endeavor he has put his hands on---barbering, massage, graphic design/apparel, book publishing. Even modeling at the legendary Bronner Brothers International Hair Show in Atlanta, Georgia. Silky also has a colorful cameo in the Ray GotIt "Stay Down" video---a street banger.

When Silky is not composing a literary gem he enjoys skateboarding---riding his electric skateboard, fishing, swimming, hiking, and exercising. He

Silky appreciates the many celebrities and experiences his new life has brought him. Change is good.

also volunteers at the Bethesda Center in Winston-Salem and does good deeds for the less fortunate faithfully. He is a native of Monroe, NC---Southside to be exact. His hometown area and all the obstacles and trauma he faced there are the influence behind his writing. That and the greats---Chester Himes, Donald Goines, Sista Soulja and Eric Jerome Dickey.

STRUGGLE STREET PUBLISHING

COMPANY

AARON "SILKY" ALLEN

BMDS BARBERING/VIP MOBILE

VIP MOBILE SPA SERVICE

WILD ASS BREE AVAILABLE ON   AMAZON NOW!!